TWINS

Published by Peter's Press
Box 2112, Revelstoke
British Columbia, Canada, VOE 2S0

Phone: (250) 837•3558
E-mail: peter revelstoke.net

National Library of Canada Cataloguing in Publication Data

Elkington, Peter W
    Twins: the story of George and Henry Hill 1930 – 1946 / Peter W. Elkington

    Includes bibliographical references.
    ISBN 0 – 9699944 – 6 – x

    I. Title.
    PS8559.L536T84 2003   C813'.54   C2003–911087–7

CREDITS

COPYEDITING
Wayne Magnuson, *Prairie House Books*, Calgary, Alberta
Jeremy Drought, *Last Impression Publishing Service*, Calgary, Alberta
INTERIOR AND COVER DESIGN
Jeremy Drought, *Last Impression Publishing Service*, Calgary, Alberta
MAPS
Marilyn Croot, *Sun Mountain Graphics*, Calgary, Alberta
COVER PHOTO
Private collection of the author.

Printed and bound in Canada by *Houghton Boston Printers & Lithographers*, Saskatoon, Saskatchewan

TWINS

The Story of George & Henry Hill
1930 – 1946

Peter W. Elkington

REVELSTOKE, BRITISH COLUMBIA

DEDICATION

To all those who lived, loved, and suffered through the nightmare of the Great Depression and World War II, I dedicate this book.

ACKNOWLEDGEMENTS

I WOULD LIKE TO ACKNOWLEDGE AND THANK THE FOLLOWING PEOPLE for their valuable help and suggestions in preparing this book for publication: Cynthia Chancellor for reading an early draft of the manuscript and providing valuable comments; Wayne Magnuson, of *Prairie House Books*, for his editorial contributions; Jeremy Drought, of *Last Impression Publishing Service*, for his additional editorial contributions, for proofreading the manuscript, and his skills in graphic design—both for the interior layout as well as the cover; Marilyn Croot, of *Sun Mountain Graphics* for the cartography; *Houghton Boston Printers & Lithographers* in Saskatoon—this is the third time they have printed a book for *Peter's Press*, and they always print and manufacture a first class book.

Peter W. Elkington
Revelstoke, BC
June 2003

CONTENTS

- Dedication v
- Acknowledgements vii
- Introduction xi

1 Germany 1918 – 1933: World War I to the Depression ... 1
2 The Twins 5
3 Germany 9
4 Ohio 17
5 George 23
6 Anna 31
7 The Herzbergs 37
8 Henry 45
9 Berlin 51
10 Homeward Bound 59
11 Ohio and the War 67
12 World War II 12
13 The Escape 81
14 George and Ann 89
15 The Pale Aunts 97
16 The Further Adventures of George and Ann 105
17 Requiem 113

- Epilogue: Personal Observations 119
- Glossary 121
- Bibliography 129

INTRODUCTION

MY FRIENDS URGED ME TO WRITE OF MY EXPERIENCES of those momentous years, 1930 to 1946. Those of us who lived through those years of and depression have vivid memories. Many of us have passed on without recording those memories, and so personal experiences are lost. History books relate events as they happened, but often the human touch is missing. It is what people felt, saw, and experienced that gives history meaning. Often you didn't realize that we were in the middle of an event, until years later—when you could look back and say I was there, and this is what happened.

In this book, I have used my experiences and those of many others, including my German classmates. This is a story about those fifteen terrible years, as seen through the eyes of people who were there. A story that could easily have happened. The places, the events, and the nightmare are all well documented. In retrospect, some events are hard to believe, for they seem so fantastic, but they happened. The Jews of Europe were slaughtered, as were many other unfortunates who did not fit the pattern. The western European democracies smiled indulgently and looked the other way, until the horror became too great. A great nation was brainwashed and hoodwinked by a twisted spellbinder and a band of thugs. France's collapse was due partly to the deep split between the Left and Right, and to inner decay and irresolution. Only Great Britain, after initial blindness, and several disastrous blunders, stood to fight, and suffered greatly. The US and the USSR were swept into the maelstrom by events beyond their control. In the end, the German High Command found themselves in the nightmare of a two-front war, which they had hoped to avoid, and which they knew they could not win. They were blinded by their own greed, and deceived by a megalomaniac.

This is a work of fiction based on well-documented historical events and personal experiences. It is the story of two countries emerging from the Great War with totally different reactions and aspirations. George and Henry Hill, seemed to me, to represent the views of both sides of the conflict. It is a story of two young men who grow up in vastly different environments. These two became very real to me, because I had experienced the same conflicts and turmoil in both countries. I have combined my experiences with those of others, along with primary source material (some of it unpublished) to create this story. It will be a familiar tale to many who lived through those extraordinary years.

Admiral Willhelm Canaris, a devout Catholic and a career naval officer, was the shadowy head of German espionage. He guided the German Army's counter-intelligence branch (The *Abwehr*). He was not an active conspirator in the attempt made to assassinate Hitler, but was active in its planning. He was a most able officer, who remained at his post until 1944, when he was arrested for treason, tortured, and executed by the Gestapo. Other historical persons make their appearance, each playing a role. The Hills and the Herzbergs are fictitious names.

Peter W. Elkington
Revelstoke, BC
June 2003

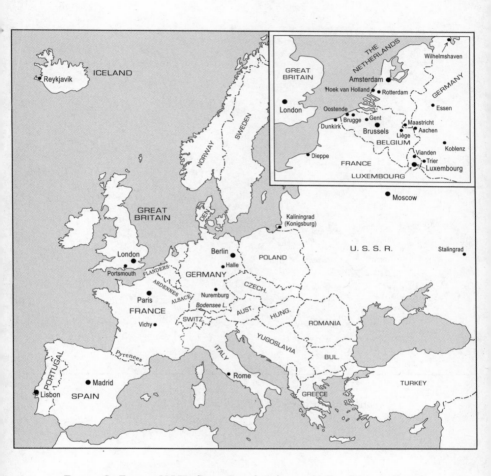

Europe & Eastern USSR (Inset Detail: Belgium, Holland, Luxembourg).

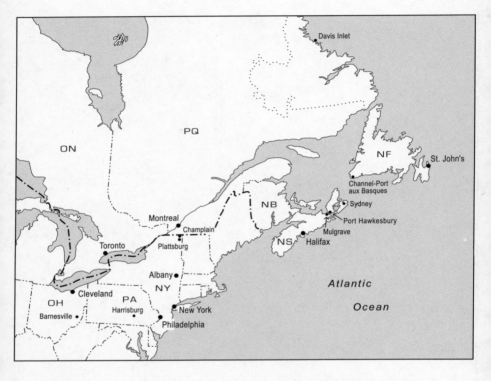

North Eastern USA & Central and Maritime Canada.

1

Germany 1918–33
World War I to the Depression

MAJOR HEINRICH HERZBERG sat in the officers' mess smoking his pipe. The morning was cool; wisps of mist floated across the valley. The Imperial armies of the Fatherland had smashed the armies of the Tsar. Major Herzberg's troops had advanced far into Russia, only to find the Russian trenches empty. Suddenly, there was nobody to fight. The Russian soldiers had shot their officers, thrown their bodies into the ditches, and left for home. Then the new Communist Government surrendered, and war on the Eastern Front was over.

Major Herzberg's orders had arrived. They were to break camp and march to Konigsburg—a three or four day trek. He expected they would be shipped to the Western Front, but he hoped for a week at home with his family. He was getting too old for active fighting. Upon their arrival in Konigsburg, General von Hindenburg awarded each of them the Iron Cross for valor.

Berlin was seething with unrest. The Kaiser, Wilhelm II, abdicated and fled the country. The Social Democrats had formed a new Republican government. The war was over and the new government signed an armistice, ending the fighting. To Heinrich Herzberg this was treason: the armies on the Eastern Front had not been defeated, nor had they surrendered.

The Allies forced terrible terms on Germany. Germans felt humiliated and bitter, and the country was burning with resentment. The French occupied the Rhineland, the British blockaded the ports, and there was widespread hunger and misery. Various protest groups sprang up around the country. The *National Sozialistische Deutsche Arbeiterpartei* or National Socialist German Workers' Party (NSDAP) attracted the most attention. Its charismatic leader preached a vision of nationalism, leadership and the greater glory of Germany. His speeches were compelling and direct. The so-called revolution, he said, was a fraud and a deception. The Social Democrats and the Communists in the new Republican Government were traitors. They caused the rampant hunger and misery of the people, decimated the currency, and destroyed German traditions and honor. His task, he said, was to restore German nationalism and honor. He ended each speech with a call to arms to abolish the Treaty of Versailles, and to resurrect a powerful, defiant Germany. National Socialism would lead them all to victory.

Heinrich Herzberg returned to his home and family a bitter man. His eldest daughter, Anna, had fallen in love and married a young American relief worker from Ohio, Peter Hill. Heinrich was more than a little resentful that they hadn't waited to be married until he returned, but the birth of twin grandsons softened the blow.

Germany had no tradition of a democratic parliamentary government. There was a general distrust of the new Republican Government among the conservative landowners, businessmen and bureaucrats. The protest organizations grew louder and more violent as the years went by.

Germany suffered two great calamities: a disastrous inflation, which wiped out the savings of the middle class, followed by an equally destructive depression, with widespread unemployment. The National Socialists were quick to blame the Republican Government for both events, and continued to preach their brand of salvation. By the end of the 1920s, they had become the second most powerful political force in the country.

Heinrich Herzberg and many other old-time Germans had grown up schooled in the traditions of authority. The National Socialists, under Adolf Hitler's leadership, was the only group who claimed they could restore Germany to its historic position of greatness. It was just a matter of time before they took control of the government.

The Germans elected former WWI General von Hindenburg, President, a conservative landowner and an avowed monarchist. Personally, Hindenburg disliked Hitler, and thought him a mere upstart, but he also distrusted the Republican Government. He hated the violence in the streets. The SA or brown shirts, Nazi semi-military storm troopers, and the organized Communist supporters, clashed at rallies, and had pitched battles in the streets. On the advice of the Chancellor, Franz von Papen, von Hindenburg was finally persuaded by fellow landowners, industrialists, and scheming politicians, to appoint Adolf Hitler as Chancellor in 1933. The bureaucrats and politicians felt they stood more of a chance of controlling Hitler if he were part of the administration, and they also hoped his appointment would stop the violence in the streets.

Once the National Socialists took political power, nothing was the same again. Hitler very quickly dispensed with constitutional restraints, effectively silenced all opposition, and successfully orchestrated the burning of the *Reichstag* (capital building)—an attack he presented as a communist plot. Hitler then used this as a pretext to call a General Election in which the police, under Göring, allowed the Nazis full play to break up the meetings of their opponents. Hitler and the NSDAP won a majority with just 37.3% of the vote.

Ohio

The war was over. The American doughboys were glad to be home. They'd had enough of trenches, mud, and lice. All they wanted was to return to a peaceful life far from the conflicts and the convoluted politics of Europe. The United States retreated into isolation protected by two vast oceans. Warren Harding and the Republicans proclaimed the return to normalcy and, for the next twelve years, the republicans controlled the political life of the country.

The war years had been good for agriculture. Prices and production were high. But following the peace, there was a drop in farm prices. While there was no longer a great demand for high agricultural production, John Hill's dairy farm had prospered. There was always a demand for dairy products. Times were good. The reconstruction of Europe began. Quaker food kitchens and relief agencies were set up in starving Germany. Peter Hill, John's eldest son, left his teaching position to undertake relief work in Germany. In 1920 he returned to Ohio, with his new wife, Anna, and infant twin boys, George and Henry. Life was peaceful and prosperous in Barnesville, Ohio.

By 1929 the economy had sputtered and crashed, leaving unemployment, bankruptcies, and farm foreclosures in its wake. There had been warning signs, but nobody had paid any attention. The financial wizards and business leaders had said that the stock market would right itself, but it didn't. Farm prices plummeted to new lows. The government floundered and did not know what to do. None of the old remedies seemed to work. The US sank further and further into the Great Depression. Businesses closed; banks called their loans and foreclosed mortgages. The unemployed and the homeless wandered the country. President Herbert Hoover and the Republicans were decisively defeated in 1933 by Franklin D. Roosevelt and the Democrats.

Two countries, with different traditions and cultures, faced the same terrible economic crisis in dramatically different ways. Ultimately, they would face each other on the battlefield in a mortal struggle.

2

The Twins

GEORGE AND HENRY HILL were identical twins; so identical that sometimes even their mother had difficulty telling them apart. They were born shortly after the end of the Great War. Their mother, Anna Herzberg, had fallen in love with and married Peter Hill, a gentle young American pacifist working in Germany with the Quaker feeding program.

Germany had lost the war. The British blockaded German ports, and there was little or no local food. The Quakers set up feeding stations and soup kitchens in various parts of the country to help provide for those in need. When the British lifted the blockade, the feeding program came to an end and Peter Hill took his young family back to Ohio.

Peter's father, John Hill, a successful dairy farmer and respected elder of the Quaker community, welcomed them back. Peter had been a teacher in the local Quaker school, and upon his return he resumed his teaching career. For the next ten years, all went well. The world was recovering from the horrors of war. Peter and Anna lived in Ohio during the winter, and spent two months each summer in Germany with Anna's parents.

The Herzbergs had a medium-sized estate in northern Germany. The Great War had not affected them too much. Heinrich Herzberg, Anna's father, a decorated veteran, had served in the Imperial Army on the Eastern Front. While he was away, Frau Herzberg had managed the farm and raised their four children. Heinrich was a conservative landowner, with little confidence in Republican politicians. Secretly, he longed for the return

5

of the monarchy. Along with everyone else, they suffered under the disastrous inflation of the 1920s.

For the Hill boys, their situation and inheritance seemed ideal. They were free to roam all over their grandfather's estate. George was the more boisterous and impulsive, while Henry, being more thoughtful, worried about the consequences of their escapades. Their adventures were forever getting them into mischief. Occasionally, their cousin Klaus visited the farm. He was a lad of medium height with a pink, cherubic face, made rounder by a crewcut. He was about five years older than the twins, with no sense of humor, and quick to point out that the twins were not true Germans. The twins thoroughly disliked him, thinking of him as a stuck-up prig.

Just before Christmas 1930, Peter Hill died of overwork and tuberculosis, leaving Anna and the boys alone. Anna took a job as a school secretary with a salary that was barely enough to support herself and the boys. The economic plight of the United States was grim, with depressed prices and low salaries. She and the boys moved into a smaller house close to the school. The summer of 1931, Anna, Henry and George made their last trip to Germany—as a family. The depression was worldwide and it had affected Germany just as badly as the United States. Many unemployed men, mostly veterans, came to the Herzberg farm seeking work.

There was no work and little money. What to do? Anna spent many an evening discussing the situation with her father. He wanted Anna to live in Germany, and bring the boys up as good Germans. He felt sure that times would get better, but Anna felt she must return to Barnesville and the rolling hills of Ohio. There she was independent, and felt closer to her memories of Peter. Besides, there was no work for women in Germany. It was finally agreed that one twin would remain with the Herzbergs, and Anna would take the other back to Ohio. The question was, which one would stay and which would return to the US? Both boys were fluently bilingual and equally at home in Germany and Ohio.

The boys were summoned to the living room to discuss the whole situation. They didn't want to be separated, but Grandfather Herzberg was adamant that one of the boys stay with them. George seemed to have a greater affinity for his grandfather's estate and German heritage, whereas Henry loved the open fields of Ohio and the freedom of thought in the United States. Henry was also very concerned about his mother. So, George was to remain in Germany with his Herzberg grandparents, and Henry and Anna would return to Barnesville.

The boys, who were inseparable, hated this. They had never been apart before, and they loved each other dearly. They always did everything and went everywhere together. On the day of departure, George was so upset he ran off by himself and would not talk to his mother or brother. Grandfather Herzberg took Anna and Henry to the station and saw them off on the train. He returned to the farm and began hunting for George, who was hiding in the cowbarn, crying because Henry had gone.

On the train, Henry was also quiet and morose, and kept saying over and over, "Poor George, Poor George." The boys had been cut in half and their pain was great. Secretly, they hated their grandfather Herzberg for insisting on the separation. They felt that he had forced their mother into making such a drastic choice.

◆ ◆ ◆

Grandfather Herzberg took a large handkerchief out of his pocket and wiped George's eyes. Then, taking him gently by the hand they walked back to the house. Grandmother was waiting in the kitchen with a steaming cup of hot chocolate for George. They sat around the kitchen table in silence, Grandfather smoking his pipe and Grandmother knitting. The cuckoo clock on the wall ticked away the minutes. There was the occasional sniffle from George. At last Grandfather spoke.

"Now Géorg, you are a true German and you must be very brave. Your Grandmother and I know that you will make us very proud. Of course you miss Henry, and he will miss you too. Someday you will understand why this had to be. Also you will understand what it means to be a true German. So, now go wash your face and hands, for supper will be ready soon."

George nodded and left the room. That night he wrote a long letter to Henry, pouring out his grief.

◆ ◆ ◆

• • •

Henry was worried and sad. He knew his brother could be stubborn. He and his mother sat on the afterdeck of the liner that was taking them away from Europe and Germany, back to the US. He told his mother about his concern for George. She nodded, and a tear rolled down her cheek, for she, too, knew of George's seeming recklessness; but she also knew how thoughtful and concerned he could be. She realized how close her boys were. Henry, the gentle one, would have been miserably unhappy had he stayed. It would be many years until she saw George again.

The Hill grandparents were at the station to welcome them home. It was a joyous reunion that night.

A week later, a letter from Henry arrived for George which, after much thought, Henry answered. He sat there a long time. At last, he took his pen and wrote a long letter to his brother in return. Thus began a correspondence that would continue until they were eventually reunited.

3

Germany

GERMANY WAS IN TURMOIL. Many veterans, including Heinrich Herzberg, felt that the Imperial Army had not been defeated, but stabbed in the back by conniving politicians—the Jews, the Socialists, and the Spartacists. The new Republican Government had dishonored Germany by accepting the Treaty of Versailles with its humiliating terms. By 1930, the National Socialist German Workers Party, under Adolf Hitler, were preaching—ever more loudly—a new vision of a greater Germany, free of the shackles of the Jews and the Communists. Hitler himself preached of a new, proud, strong Germany, an equal among the other nations of Europe, with employment for all. This appealed to the unemployed, the poor, and the destitute veterans.

Veterans in shabby coats often came to the Herzberg farm to spend the evening, and to extol the virtues of National Socialism. They handed out copies of the party newspaper, *Der Angriff* (The Attack), and all carried well-worn copies of Hitler's book, *Mein Kampf* (My Struggle). They quoted endlessly from *Mein Kampf* to bolster their message of salvation. Anna would go to the kitchen rather than argue or listen to the twisted logic of the Nazis. Her father, although not an active party member, had quietly begun to agree with them. Hitler preached all of the right ideas to make Germany great again. He did not trust the Republican Government because they had badly mishandled the finances of the nation. First the devastating inflation that had destroyed the middle class; then the depression, with its massive unemployment. However, he was optimistic that the National

Socialist German Workers Party, if elected, could save the country from the Jews, Communists, and Social Democrats before it was too late.

At the supper table, Grandfather Herzberg would pontificate on the glories of National Socialism, and the wonders that Adolf Hitler preached. He urged Anna to listen to reason. "Germany," he said with pride, "is an ideal place to bring up the boys." Anna sat and listened, but longed for her home in Ohio. In August 1931 she and Henry left for the United States.

• • •

November was a beautiful month in northern Germany. There was frost, and the ground was crisp underfoot. November 16 was a special day for George. He and his Grandfather were going to Berlin. Grandfather said he had party business to attend to. Grandmother served George's favorite breakfast: potato pancakes and sausages. For George, this was an adventure; he had never been to Berlin. They drove along the road in Grandfather's ancient car and, as they passed each field, the workers stopped and waved.

Through the Brandenburger Tor they drove, and parked the car on Prinze Louis Ferdinandstrasse, then walked down the Unter den Linden. Everything was so new to George. Berlin was a big city. He saw a squad of men dressed in brown shirts marching toward them and, as they came, they sang stirring martial songs. George watched as they marched by. Suddenly, from a side street, there burst a rowdy group of teenagers and young men, throwing stones, bottles, and debris at the marchers. The brown shirts turned and attacked viciously, swinging their truncheons and dispersing the rowdies. Several young men lay bleeding in the gutter. The policeman on the corner paid no attention whatever; in fact, he turned and looked the other way. Grandfather was disgusted. The rabble, he said, were all communists, then added, "What Germany needs is discipline and order!"

"Who were the marching men, Grandfather?" George asked.

"They are the army of the new party—the party of law and order. When they form the government, you'll see."

"Who is going to help those people in the gutter?"

"Never mind," said his grandfather. "They are only communists or Jews."

George was very puzzled by all this. He had never seen his grandfather so angry. It was all very bewildering, and a little disturbing. George wondered what Henry would think. Without further discussion, George and his grandfather continued walking down the avenue. They turned into a new office building and took the elevator upstairs. Grandfather opened the door and they saw a man in a brown shirt sitting behind a desk. Heinrich saluted. It was not the usual military salute, but the right arm extended straight out. In the corner of the room was the new party flag, blood red with a black swastika in a white field in the middle. On the wall, was a full-length picture of Adolf Hitler, the party leader. Grandfather introduced George, with handshakes all around. Then Grandfather and the man in the brown shirt talked party business, which George didn't really understand. They talked for over an hour. When they finally stood, the men saluted again. George and his grandfather left, crossing the street to the Heidelberg Hof for lunch. During lunch, a number men, some dressed in brown shirts, stopped at their table for a chat with Grandfather.

It had been an exciting day. At supper, George couldn't contain his excitement in telling of their adventures. He wondered about the men in the brown shirts. He thought they were awfully rough, the way they smashed heads with their truncheons. He wasn't sure he wanted anything to do with them. Grandfather was very pleased with the way the day had gone. He smiled at Grandmother, who nodded her approval. That night George wrote a letter Henry a long letter, full of the experiences of the day and expressing his concerns and doubts.

At school the next day, some of George's classmates told of the marching brown shirts, and how proud they were of them. George didn't say anything.

◆ ◆ ◆

January 31, 1933 began as any other day on the farm. George walked to school across the frozen fields. He saw people rushing about, but paid little attention. The schoolmaster stood at the front of the room. He looked very solemn and a little sad, not his usual outgoing self. George spoke to him, but he just shook his head and turned away. It was a sober day at school. George wondered why. He walked home along the snowy road swinging his book bag slowly, back and forth. He hoped there would be a letter from Henry. He missed Henry. What would he do if he were here, George wondered. He came around the hill and saw the new blood-red flag of Germany hanging over the balcony of his grandfather's house. He opened the back door and walked into the kitchen. Grandmother, who was working at the stove, turned and threw her arms around him and hugged him. Her eyes shone brightly as she spoke.

"Oh, Géorg! Great news! Our President, von Hindenburg, has just appointed Herr Hitler Chancellor. Now the New Order can begin. Heil Hitler!"

George was amazed and didn't quite understand. Then Grandfather rushed in, saluted, and shouted, "Heil Hitler! You saw the new flag. Isn't it beautiful!"

George nodded, but he actually thought it was ugly.

So began the New Order, and everything changed. Within two weeks they had a new schoolmaster, an ex-army major who demanded obedience and order. George walked to school every day with his friend Werner, the son of a Jewish shopkeeper. Werner wanted to practice his English so the two boys would talk in English on their way to school. The schoolmaster heard them and ordered George to come forward; then he caned him in front of the whole class. He ordered him, as a good German, never to speak English again. George was hurt and humiliated, but said nothing. Werner's father's store was trashed by the SA (the brown shirts) and the family driven out of town. At supper George told his grandparents what had happened.

Grandfather shook his finger at George. "You must never, never disobey the schoolmaster. You are a good German. Remember that!"

Grandmother added, "After all, the Jews are inferior people, and not really Germans."

That night George wrote a very unhappy letter to Henry. He realized that from now on he had to be very careful about what he said and did.

◆ ◆ ◆

The following summer of 1934 passed peacefully enough. President von Hindenburg died, and Hitler assumed full command of the country. School opened in September. On the dais stood the schoolmaster and a high ranking member of the National Socialist Party, in full uniform. The party official stepped forward, saluted and said, "Heil Hitler! The Führer is delighted to tell you that Géorg Herzberg has been selected to go to the language school. Heil Hitler!"

George was delighted. He stood up and saluted. That night, at supper, he told his grandparents of his selection. Grandfather nodded and said he was sure that George had been selected because of his talent. Now he must serve the Fuhrer and the Party faithfully and well. Twice a week George went across town to the language school. A unit of the Hitler Youth was organized in the school. All the boys had to join, and swear an oath of allegiance to Hitler and the Party, as Hitler had said in a speech:

You, my youth, are our nation's most precious guarantee for a great future. You are destined to be the leaders of a glorious new order under National Socialism. You, my youth, must never forget that one day you will rule the world.

This was heady stuff for adolescent school boys. They all lined up and marched to the front of the room. Each took hold of the new German flag and swore the following oath:

I promise, in the Hitler Youth, to do my duty at all times in love and faithfulness to help the Fuhrer so help me God. Our banner means more to me than death.

George took the oath because, to refuse would have been utter folly. However, there were niggling doubts in the back of his mind.

The whole emphasis of the school changed. All subject matter was rewritten, slanted and biased toward the glories of National Socialism. Books—even those only slightly antigovernment in their bias—were destroyed or banned. New textbooks reflected the power and the glory of the new Germany. Books by Jewish authors were burned, and Jewish instructors were fired. Jewish children were forced to attend a very inferior school at the edge of town. For after all, as Grandmother said, Jews weren't true Germans, and shouldn't be allowed to associate with Germans.

George had started down a very slippery slope. Where it would lead, he didn't know. He only knew that it was the only thing he could do. He confided his doubts to Henry, but even these thoughts could not be expressed openly. George could no longer write to Henry in English or German, because their letters were censored. So they devised a coded language known only to themselves.

The new government put the unemployed back to work, mostly in armament plants, or building super highways. Grandfather Herzberg now had help on the estate. Wages were set at the lowest possible level. The undesirables—Communists and Jews—simply vanished from everyday life. No one bothered to find out where they had gone. You didn't ask, it was too dangerous. Hitler and the Party were all-powerful. George came home from school one day to find Grandfather storming around the kitchen. Hitler, he said, had smashed the corrupt SA (brown shirts/storm troopers) leadership—the traitors. They and other subversives had, according to all reports, planed to overthrow the Government. Hitler had discovered their plot, and personally shot the ringleaders. He had saved the Reich. Germany was now on the path to greatness. With the destruction of the SA, the army became one of the chief instruments of power.

For the balance of his school year and the whole of the next year George transferred to a higher language school in another town, so he came home only on weekends. After two years of intensive language study and party indoctrination, he graduated at the head of his class. The Herzberg grandparents were very proud of him. To them, he was a good Nazi and a good German; but in the back of George's mind were many lingering doubts, and he wasn't so sure.

That summer, between graduation and army training, George and a classmate received permission to go hiking around Germany, provided they checked with the police once a week. Just before they were to leave, his companion fell seriously ill, so George continued as planned by himself. He wanted to see the country and meet as many of the common people as he could. He talked to tourists, to farmers, and to workers. He hiked through the mountains and even stayed at a much-neglected monastery on Bodensee (Lake of Constance). On a day-trip into Switzerland, he mailed a small packet of letters to Henry. The Nazi Party was omnipresent and the doctrine of the National Socialists was everywhere. The press and the radio constantly trumpeted the party line, even on the street corners. The vicious anti-Semitic newspaper, *Der Strumer*, was on display. It was forbidden to listen to foreign radio broadcasts.

The question asked of George most often was, *Why does the rest of the world hate Germany? We are only trying to live in peace.* George had no real answer. Underneath all this, a feeling of fear, frustration, and grave doubt troubled him. He was unsure about the future of Germany, and he shared his thoughts with Henry. One thing he had learned on the trip was to keep his mouth shut. "You must never let anyone know what you are thinking, for it could be very dangerous," he wrote in their secret code.

The last leg of his journey took him through the Black Forest, and down the Rhine Valley. He traveled by coal barge down the Rhine to Essen, and finally home by train. He said goodbye to his grandparents and left for six months in the Labor Service, and then two years of basic training in the army.

4

Ohio

ANNA AND HENRY RETURNED TO THEIR HOME IN AMERICA in the fall of 1931. Ohio is lovely rolling country with small farms, an area of ample rainfall and heavy winter snows. One year after the depression began, the economic situation in Ohio was desperate. There was no work for the unemployed, and farm prices had fallen to ridiculously low levels. A freight car full of melons sold on the Cleveland market for $3.00, of which the farmer received $2.00. Milk was twenty-five cents a quart at the local creamery. It didn't pay to ship it.

Anna still had her job, but it paid very little. For Henry, there was only one pair of shoes a year, and Anna patched his clothes over and over again. Sometimes a parent would leave a chicken or perhaps some vegetables in the school office, to help pay for school expenses. These gifts the staff divided among themselves. There was very little money, but nobody in the community starved. After school Henry worked for an old Quaker couple. He did their chores and other tasks the old couple could no longer undertake for themselves. They paid him with eggs, and vegetables from their garden. The Hill grandparents still kept their herd of dairy cows and sold their milk locally.

Groups of desperate men came into the town on the train looking for work, but there was none. The Quaker Meeting, out of love and compassion, ran a soup kitchen six days a week. They fed every destitute person that came by, at least one good meal a day. When these men moved on, other job hunters took their place. The town developed a reputation for its soup kitchen. Word went out that you could always get a hot meal there, except on Sundays. Henry worked Saturdays in the kitchen, and at the end of the day he took home a pot of soup for their supper. The Quaker Meeting was often asked why they fed the destitute, and the reply was always the same: *These are hungry people.*

Henry was deeply distressed by these poor people seeking work. Sometimes he saw women and children who had been evicted from their homes and had no place to go. The Meeting tried its best to take care them, but they did not always succeed. Henry asked his mother where the system had failed. She had no answer. On Sunday, after Quaker meeting, Henry and Anna would walk to the Hill's farm for dinner. The Hills loved their daughter-in-law and it distressed them that she worked so hard, but when asked, she would answer, "Peter would have wished it."

Henry often wondered what George was doing, and looked forward to his letters. George's life seemed so exciting, but Henry worried that George was getting too involved. The German Government and the Nazi Party were destroying all opposition. Anna could not understand her parents. Why had they embraced the National Socialist Party so completely?

The new President of the United States promised a *New Deal* for the country. His ringing call that *Americans have nothing to fear but fear itself* was a challenge to all. The depression continued, with more layoffs, more bankruptcies, more desperation.

One day, down by the railroad, Henry met a young lad his own age. They sat on the bank overlooking the tracks and talked. The boy seemed angry and very resentful. "We lived in a comfortable downstairs apartment in the city," he said. "My father had a good job in a hardware store. I went to school. A year ago my father was laid off, and the store closed. We had no money. Father went out every day to look for work, but there was none. One day the landlord came by and told us that we had to pay the back rent or be evicted. We had no money. A month later the sheriff came and turned us out of the apartment. All our belongings were piled on the street. I had to quit school in order to find work, which was tough. My parents did find a very small apartment, just enough room for two. Mother got a job sewing for a clothing jobber at a nickel a garment. I had no place to stay, so I hit the road. You wonder why I'm angry? I haven't slept in a bed for over a year, and I'm lucky if I get one meal a day. What clothes I have, I steal. Tomorrow, I'll move on west, maybe there is work out there."

They talked for a long time. Henry took him to the soup kitchen for a hot meal and then said goodbye. At supper Henry and his mother agreed that the depression was so unfair.

The government didn't seem to know what to do. State governments had no money for relief projects. The old remedies failed. There was a widespread belief that welfare was an admission of failure. It meant that you couldn't manage your own life or support your family, and no man wanted that, but you couldn't let your family starve. In many cities men were forced to leave home so their wives and children could apply for welfare.

The depression was going to last a long time. It was time for new ideas and new directions. The federal government started two new programs: one to build roads and new buildings; and the other, a Civilian Conservation Corps, to build parks and recreation areas. Those enlisting with CCC received clothes, three meals a day, housing, plus a minimum wage, of which a portion went home to their families. This was definitely better than nothing. The business community roundly criticized the federal government for what they considered a pampering of the unemployed. On the other hand, they couldn't let people starve.

George's letters described a country vastly different from the one Henry knew. Germany seemed prosperous. There was no unemployment. All the destitute and people on welfare, George said, had been rounded up and put to work. The undesirables, Communists, and those opposed to the government, disappeared. Henry read between the lines and sensed that the German people were paying a very heavy price for their prosperity. George commented on the Jewish situation, and although he didn't approve, he had to be very careful not to voice his opposition too loudly. Henry's letters described what was happening in their town, and confided his hopes, fears and doubts to George. The Germans censured all mail going in and out of country, so the boys used a special language all their own, which even their mother couldn't decipher. In this way they could write freely back and forth.

The depression got worse. Ohio was suffering from a prolonged drought. The midwest faced wild dust storms; the east endured severe winters. Desperate people migrated west to look for work, but there was none. The Quaker soup kitchen continued to run even though at times it looked hopeless. Henry graduated from high school and went to work on his grandfather's farm.

One morning, Henry and his grandfather were working in the fields. Grandmother had gone to town to get supplies and have lunch with Anna. The men returned to house for lunch and found an intruder going through the kitchen cupboards.

Grandfather Hill spoke in a very quiet voice. "Friend, is thee looking for something?"

Surprised, the intruder turned and pulled a pistol out of his pocket. Grandfather walked over to him and, putting his hand on the intruder's arm, continued. "Put that away before thee does harm to either thyself or others. Perhaps we can help thee. I see that thee has taken some silver. Thee must have a greater need for it than we. Come, sit down, thee can share lunch with us."

The intruder looked a little bewildered, but did as he was told. Henry served the soup and bread that Grandmother had left for them. Grandfather Hill gave thanks, praying that their guest would be blessed. As they ate lunch, the intruder began to talk. He told them his name was John and how he'd lost his job when the factory closed; how he'd left his family so that his wife could qualify for welfare. Desperate and hungry, he'd walked from a neighboring town. He said this lunch was his first meal in three days. Grandfather said that he could use an extra hand in the field that afternoon, and would be happy to pay him. The three worked in the field all afternoon. At the end of the day Grandfather paid him for a full day's work.

Grandmother, who had returned from town, came out of the house and handed the visitor a towel. "After thee has washed up, we would welcome thee to share supper with us." Then Grandfather told John he could sleep in the barn and sent Henry to fetch a blanket and pillow.

In the morning, after having breakfast together, John went on his way. Henry asked his Grandfather about their encounter with John. Grandfather simply quoted the Bible: "I was in need and ye ministered unto me." Later, Henry wrote to George telling of their grandparents' love and compassion for the destitute.

As Henry walked home that evening, he thought about all that had happened, and wondered if he could be as loving and compassionate as his grandparents. He told his Mother about John's surprise visit to the farm. She listened, smiled, and thought to herself, *How like his father he is.* Then she thought of George and began to worry. She asked Henry what he had heard, and Henry translated the last letter he had received from George. What he shared worried Anna even more.

5

George

THE LABOR CORPS BORED GEORGE. He didn't mind the hard work, he was used to that. It was the military drill and marching that bothered him, and the endless, stupid Nazi indoctrination. He put up with it, because there was no way he could object. His six-month tour of duty went by quickly. He went home for two weeks before reporting to the army. He had no choice, really, for the Nazi government would tolerate no opposition or dissent. He remembered his father's gentle pacifism, and wondered what Henry would do if faced with the same choice.

After six months of basic training, George, already fluent in English and French, was assigned to the army's advanced language school. He had been there about six months when the superintendent summoned him to his office. He entered and saluted the officer, then stood awaiting orders. Seated to the side of the room was a frail looking, grey-haired gentleman in a large, naval greatcoat buttoned up to his chin. He looked at George, then dismissed the superintendent with a wave of his hand.

The naval officer interrogated George for three hours in three languages. He would switch in the middle of a sentence from one language to another. George didn't miss a beat and answered all the questions in whatever language he was asked. At last the grey-haired man nodded, and dismissed George.

The next day the superintendent called George down to the office again. He stood behind his desk bursting with pride: one of his students had been chosen for advancement. The *Abwehr* had selected George to attend its espionage school. George was to report to the *Abwehr* in Berlin by the end of the week.

Dressed in his best uniform, George reported for duty and was directed to an office on the top floor of the *OKW* Building (headquarters of the Commander-in-Chief of the German Armed Forces). He knocked on an unmarked door, went in and saluted. It was a very plain office. There was a desk and several chairs, a blanket-covered army cot in one corner of the room, and an inscribed picture of Franco on the wall. Seated behind the desk was the old gentleman who had interviewed him, this time in full uniform: Admiral Wilhelm Canaris, head of the Army Counter Intelligence Service, the *Abwehr*. The Admiral waved him to a seat.

"I like you, boy. I was impressed by the way you handled yourself the other day. I want you on my staff. You are to be assigned to the espionage school and then you are to come back here. Do you understand?"

George felt flattered that the Admiral had chosen him over the others. The Admiral seemed so different from all the other officers he saw. Certainly different from the arrogant Gestapo, and the haughty army generals.

The Admiral went on, "Now tell me about your family. I know who your grandparents are, but what about your father and mother, and do you have any brothers or sisters?"

"Yes, I have an identical twin brother, Henry, who lives with my mother in Ohio. Mother and father married after the Great War. Father was here with the Quaker feeding program, but he died of tuberculosis in 1930 and mother was unable to support both of us. Grandfather Herzberg wanted us all to stay in Germany, but Mother insisted on returning to Ohio. Grandfather Herzberg insisted that I stay with them. Henry went back to Ohio with Mother. He is also fluently bilingual, and I miss him." George had never talked like this to anybody but family.

The Admiral nodded, sat silent for awhile, then said, "Thank you, I would like to meet your brother sometime. Now, go downstairs and get your new uniform, then check into your lodgings. I'll see you tomorrow morning before you go off to school."

George stood and started to salute, but the Admiral stopped him with a curt remark, saying that saluting in his office was unnecessary.

There was something different about the Admiral and the *Abwehr*. George could not put his finger on it, but it was different. He went downstairs, collected his new uniform and caught the tram to his new boarding house. A round motherly widow was in charge of the house and took a personal interest in all her boarders. George had a pleasant room on the top floor overlooking the Tiergarten, Berlin's great Central Park and Zoo.

He sat looking out the window, thinking about his good luck. Down below he saw a group of SA (brown shirts/storm troopers) ruffians forcing Jewish men and women to scrub the sidewalk with tooth brushes. They were laughing and jeering. Now and then a guard would kick a Jew down or throw dirt on the sidewalk, and the other troopers would laugh. Later he wrote a long letter to Henry, describing the scene. He knew what he was doing was dangerous, but he had confidence in their secret language.

The landlady rang the bell for supper. George folded his letter, put it in an envelope, then in his pocket and went downstairs. All the boarders, a dozen or so, representing the various services of the Reich, gathered in the dining room for an ample meal of meat, boiled potatoes, overcooked cabbage and, for dessert, fruit compote.

The next morning George entered the *OKW* Building. The lobby was full of high-ranking generals in full uniform. Nobody paid any attention to him as he slipped quietly around the edges and up the stairs. He knocked on the Admiral's door and was bidden to come in. The Admiral sat behind his desk looking very sad.

"George, you saw all those puffed-up generals downstairs? They are all going to hear their death sentences today. The Fuhrer has called the high command together. He is going to give them orders to prepare for war. We are not prepared for war," he sighed and shook his head, "but we have a duty to perform. Here is your assignment: Go to the espionage school. Learn all you can, as fast as you can, and keep your mouth shut. I am going need your skills, perhaps sooner than we think. You are one of very few in the *Abwehr* who is completely fluent in three languages. My best wishes go with you." They saluted, navy fashion.

George left the *OKW* Building and caught a tram to the outskirts of the city. The espionage school, run by the *Abwehr*, was housed in the confiscated chateau of a Jewish businessman. George handed his orders to the Kommandant and was assigned to a language unit. The weeks and months flew by.

The Nazi generals prepared for a war with total confidence of victory, but military intelligence felt that the country itself was unprepared. There was full employment, and the armament factories were operating at full production. Hitler had repudiated the Treaty of Versailles, and reestablished military service. Still, Germany was far behind the other nations of Europe in military readiness.

• • •

In the spring of 1938 the army marched into Austria without a shot being fired. The German airwaves were full of triumphant statements and news of the enthusiastic welcome the Austrian people gave the German troops. They announced the overthrow of the corrupt Austrian government by the might of the army and the power of Hitler's Nationalist Socialist Party. According to German propaganda, the new Austrian government of Nazis and other sympathizers had invited the German army to restore peace and order. The Gestapo quickly rounded up the Jews, socialists and other undesirables, and sent them all to concentration camps and eventual death.

One morning, the Kommandant of the espionage school handed George a note. He was to report to the Admiral immediately. George hurried downtown to the OKW Building and reported to the Admiral. He had barely taken a seat when the Admiral began.

"George, you don't believe all that propaganda the papers are printing, do you? You know perfectly well that there was a great deal of preparation for that invasion. The Fuhrer wants to rationalize the invasion. He wants the German people to believe that the incorporation of Austria into the Reich was the Austrians' idea. Unfortunately, the masses of Germans believe what they read in the papers and hear on the radio. Dr. Göbbels sees to that." He found a file on his desk and looked up again.

"I'm sending you to France. You have applied to St. Cyr, the French military academy, for junior officer's training, and you have already been accepted. It is a very intensive six months of training. You will be the talented son of a French peasant from Alsace, who hates the Germans. You are to report to St. Cyr next week. I don't have to tell you to keep your eyes and ears open. I'll expect a full report on the state of French preparedness when you return. Here are all your papers, including a passport. Take care." And much to George's surprise, the Admiral added, "And may God Bless you." Admiral Canaris was a devout Catholic.

George left for France the next day. A letter from the *Abwehr* satisfied the German border guards. To the French customs agents, his French passport showed he was a French student returning from a late spring ski tour in the Bavarian alps. George wondered how he was going to get back into Germany, but the Admiral said not to worry. Later that week he reported to the military academy at St. Cyr. He immediately enrolled in a class for junior officer trainees.

It was six months of very difficult training. George graduated head of his class, as a junior lieutenant in the French army. His brilliance of thought had been remarked upon by senior officers. For his achievement, he was attached to the diplomatic delegation that was going to the international conference in Munich.

Early one morning, the Munich police found the disfigured body of what they believed to be a young French officer outside a house of ill repute. The French delegation was irate and demanded an explanation. The local police investigated and concluded that the young officer had been murdered, possibly a crime of passion. They stressed the point that the young officer had no business in that part of town, in any case.

George, dressed as a sober young German businessman, stepped onto the platform of the Friedrichstrasse Bahnhof, safely back in Berlin. The Admiral sat behind his desk and listened very carefully as George gave his report. Occasionally he asked a question or took a few notes, but mainly he just listened. George continued to talk. Lunch was brought in. They continued their conversation well into the afternoon.

"The French army's whole strategy," George was saying, "is based on defense. They are planning for a war like the Great War. They feel that the Maginot Line is so strong that it will stop any German invasion. However," he went on, "the Maginot Line only went part way. The

Belgian-France frontier was still unprotected, and the whole French command structure was incompetent. Their thinking is still based on the Great War, and they don't see beyond 1918. Their command structure is totally unprepared for modern warfare. They have a handful of modern fighter planes, very few bombers, a few good tanks, but no organization. There is a dearth of modern communications equipment—no radios, no telephones—and they rely on hand-delivered orders. They still use a horse cavalry. Germany need not worry about France, militarily. Their infantry divisions are hollow and ill-equipped. They will not fight. The only bright aspect of the French army is the younger officers, who are competent and intelligent. However, their ideas and suggestions are systematically ignored by the conservative, entrenched high command."

After listening to George's report the Admiral said, "George, go home to your grandparents. Go and work on the farm, rest for a couple of weeks, away from all this. You have done more than I expected and I am very proud of you. If anyone asks where you have been, just say that you've been in training. Nobody knows you work for the *Abwehr*, and we will keep it that way." He rose, walked around his desk and shook George by the hand.

That night, in his attic room, George wrote to Henry and tried to put into words what it was like to lead a double life. He hated it, but what could he do? He felt trapped in a terrible system. He knew he lived a charmed life, under the protection of the Admiral, but how long this was going to last, he didn't know. Life in Germany could be dangerous.

The next morning George was astonished, as he walked down the street. Every Jewish shop on the street had been smashed and vandalized. The streets were filled with piles of broken glass and destroyed property. Jewish shops, synagogues and businesses all over Germany had been smashed and looted, or burned. George watched the reaction of the passersby: some shook their heads in disbelief, some refused to look, and others smirked and gloated. The papers and radio hailed this destruction as the heroic reaction of the German people to a dastardly attack by a young Polish Jew on a diplomatic officer in Paris.

The *Völkischer Beobachter*, (the *People's Observer* – the official government-controlled newspaper of the Third Reich), heralded a new master plan for all German Jews:

"The Jews are to be divided into three groups. The young and the able-bodied men are to be put into a type of work camp to labor for the Reich on various projects. The second group, consisting of the infirm, old, and poor, are to be segregated into a poorhouse type of barracks, paid for with money taken from the sale of Jewish businesses. The third group, comprised manly of wealthy Jews, would be placed in a settlement of their own, apart from other Germans, at their own expense."

This, the paper said, would help to solve the Jewish problem for all time. It depressed George, for he could see nothing but trouble.

• • •

George packed his bag and took the train back to the farm. As he walked into the farmyard he saw the Nazi swastika flying from a permanent flagpole. That night, in the kitchen, Grandfather Herzberg heralded the new day for Germany, with the banning of all Jews from the mainstream of German life. The Jew, he said, not only polluted society, but were a blot on the German soul. He also praised sterilizing the mentally deficient and euthanizing old and infirm mental patients.

This was barbaric! George just listened. Grandfather rejoiced that his other grandson, Klaus, had risen in the ranks of the SS. Grandfather's prejudice oppressed him. George picked up Henry's letters and went upstairs. He sat at the desk and wrote to Henry, expressing his doubts and fears. George knew that while he worked on the farm he would have to keep such thoughts to himself. It would not do to antagonize his fanatical grandparents.

6

Anna

THE CHERRY BLOSSOMS WERE IN FULL BLOOM all around the tidal basin in Washington, DC. It was a lovely spring day. The public gardens were full of varicolored flowers. Washington, in all its fresh finery was just emerging from a dull, dreary winter.

On a side street, in a temporary office building constructed during World War I, the Federal Bureau of Investigation (FBI) had its office. That morning, they had received a coded message from their agent in Germany. It covered many topics. Toward the end of the dispatch, there was mention of a rising young member of the *Abwehr*, George Hill. He was a shadowy figure who seemed to be an active member of Admiral Canaris's staff. His mother, Anna Hill, nee Herzberg, lived in Barnesville, Ohio, with her other son. This information was noted and forwarded to the Cleveland office, with orders to investigate.

Several days later, the FBI intercepted a letter addressed to Henry Hill, George's brother. It was in code, which the FBI could not break. The FBI decided to act. Two agents were dispatched to Barnesville to check on Mrs. Hill and her son. They found that she was the secretary in the local Quaker school.

Barnesville was a small farming community in the rolling farm country of Ohio. It was a division point on the Pennsylvania railroad's main line to St. Louis. Quakers made up the majority of the town's population. There was a Quaker Meeting, which drew from the town and the surrounding area, two or three other small Protestant churches and a hotel; there was also a thriving Quaker school—kindergarten through grade twelve. Children who didn't go to the Quaker school attended a small public school.

Anna was just finishing her day's work at the school when two men came into the office. She had noticed them a couple of days before, but had thought nothing of it.

"Are you Anna Herzberg? We're from the FBI."

"Yes," she replied, "that was my maiden name; now I am Anna Hill."

"No matter, you are under arrest. Would you please come with us."

Anna protested that there must be some mistake, but the men just shook their heads. They would not allow her to phone either her father-in-law or Henry. Anna put on her hat and coat, and picked up her purse. They handcuffed her and manhandled her into a waiting car. Henry came down the street just in time to see his mother being pushed into the car. He rushed up and protested.

"Shut up," they told him. "She is a spy, and we're going to deport her."

The agent behind the wheel slammed the car door and drove away. Henry ran out to his grandfather's farm and told Grandfather Hill what had happened. Grandfather listened very carefully, went into his office, gathered up Anna's naturalization papers, kissed his wife and drove with Henry into Cleveland.

Anna was in the county jail, pending a deportation hearing. They had taken away her hat, purse and shoes, and thrown her into the women's drunk tank. Anna sat huddled in a corner, weeping quietly. A very drunk old lady sat down beside her and tried to comfort her, but to no avail. Oh, the humiliation of it all!

Grandfather Hill and Henry walked into the FBI office and asked to see the agent in charge. There was some argument with the duty officer, but Grandfather in his quiet way, insisted. They were ushered into a small drab office and told to wait. Presently the agent came in and asked what they wanted. Grandfather answered.

"My name is John Hill. I am a dairy farmer from Barnesville, and this is my grandson Henry Hill. I am here to arrange for the release of my daughter-in-law."

"But Mr. Hill, she is a spy, and is to be deported."

"Thee is mistaken, she is not a spy. She is an American citizen and has lived in Barnesville since 1920. Here are her papers."

"We know she is a spy, because her son is a Nazi spy, and he writes letters in code."

Henry laughed quietly, and the agent turned on him.

"What do you know about this? Does your brother live in Germany?"

"Yes, and he writes to me. If you will show me the letter I will be glad to translate it for you."

"But," the agent shot back, "it's in code."

Henry said that was true. It was a code that he and his brother had devised so they could write to each other without fear of someone else reading their letters. The agent frowned and sent another agent to fetch the letter. It was George's latest. Henry took it and began translating it, editing as he read.

The agent was very interested in George's description of the Jews being made to scrub the sidewalk with tooth brushes. He scratched his head. "I heard they did this, but I didn't believe it. It's barbaric!"

"That's the way they treat all the Jews," Henry said, carefully folding the letter, returning it to its envelope and handed it back to the agent. "I'd like my brother's letter back, when you're finished with it," said Henry.

"We'll see what we can do about that later," said the agent. "For the time being, we'd like to keep it in on file. Now, tell me Henry, do you think your brother is a Nazi?"

"Yes, he is, because he had to join the party or risk being sent to a concentration camp or worse—perhaps shot as a traitor towards the New Order."

"Is he a spy?"

"I don't think so, but I really don't know. He is studying at the advanced language school."

"Does he work for the *Abwehr*?"

"I don't know for sure, he's never said directly."

The agent wanted to know why George was in Germany but Anna and Henry were in Ohio. Grandfather Hill patiently explained the whole situation, from the Quaker Feeding Program in 1918 to the present. When his eldest son, Peter Hill, died, Anna could not support both boys. It was decided that George would stay with his Herzberg grandparents, while Anna and Henry returned to Ohio. Anna did not want to live in Germany, and she would have preferred to raise both boys in Ohio, but that couldn't be. All this was duly recorded. The agent excused himself and left the room. Shortly he returned with another agent, who wanted to hear the whole story again. After the retelling of the story, both agents appeared to be satisfied, and produced an order for Anna's release.

"Well, Mr. Hill, I see we didn't know all the facts in this case."

Grandfather, Henry, and the first agent walked across the street to the county jail and gave the order for Anna's release to the deputy on duty. When Anna came out, they could see that she hadn't had much rest and had been crying. Her hair and clothes were in disarray. She rushed into grandfather Hill's arms and burst into tears. Grandfather Hill soothed and comforted her. The agent looked embarrassed, and drew a long breath.

"Mr. Hill, I will put your daughter-in-law in your care. Technically, she is still under surveillance. If you can guarantee that your daughter-in-law is no spy and that the letters your grandson receives from his brother are as he says, then we will set this case aside, but we should like to retain Mrs. Hill's passport for the time being."

Grandfather Hill nodded. "Thee need have no worry, friend, about either my daughter-in-law or my grandson."

"Good," the agent replied. "Then you are free to go."

Anna collected her belongings, put on her shoes and they walked to the car. It was a long somber drive back to the farm. Anna, shaken by the whole experience, wept and then slept most of the way. She knew that she may never see her parents again. When they arrived at their farm Grandmother Hill embraced Anna and took her upstairs so she could have a warm bath, wash her hair, and put on some clean clothes.

Later that night, Anna wrote a long emotional letter to her parents, bidding them goodbye. A month later, a vicious letter arrived from her father. He blamed Anna for not having listened to his advice. It was all her fault that she now lived in a Jew-dominated country that had no respect for human rights. What kind of a society was Henry growing up in, with its mongrel values? Had she stayed in Germany the boys would have been proper Germans in a pure Aryan society, free from Jewish domination and the mixing of mongrel races. According to him, Germany was now a land of peace, freedom, prosperity, and good order, thanks to Hitler and the National Socialists. Thank goodness George had been enlightened by the party and was doing so well. In the final paragraph of his letter he dismissed Anna from his life. "You are," he wrote, "no longer a good German worthy of my respect."

Anna wept, for she loved her parents. It took a long time to recover from this hammer-blow. It was only with the steadfast support of Henry and her mother and father-in-law that she was able to move forward with her life. A month or so later, one of the FBI agents dropped by the school office to see Anna. He wanted to know how she was doing. Anna showed him her father's letter and said how crushed she had been, but that she was now resigned to put it behind her as she had nothing but the future to live for. She didn't consider herself German any more. She explained to the agent how she had fallen in love with the gentle Peter Hill. His pacifism and loving concern for people had become for her an anchor. Since his death she had tried to instill those qualities in her son Henry. She only regretted that George was not here too. The agent left, much impressed.

• • •

Anna was a very pretty young widow. Peter Hill's younger brother, John Jr., was a successful farmer in the area. His beautiful young wife had passed away over a year ago, leaving him with a very young daughter, Emily. John proposed to Anna. In the late spring, they married in the Quaker Meeting House, after the manner of Friends. It was a joyous wedding. The whole Quaker community came to celebrate. Henry was very pleased, for he liked his Uncle John very much. He wrote the happy news to George. Anna sold her house in town and moved out to John's farm. She was very happy to have a little daughter to bring up, but she worried about George. She hoped and prayed that his close ties with Henry would save him from catastrophe. As long she was under FBI surveillance, she could not write to him, but Henry could and did. Still she worried.

7

The Herzbergs

THERE WERE TWO LETTERS FROM HENRY waiting for George when he returned to the Herzberg farm. One told of his mother's arrest and detention, and the other of her marriage to John Hill Jr., which pleased George very much. At breakfast, George told his grandparents of Anna's troubles.

Grandfather Herzberg turned red in the face, pounded his fist on the table and shouted, "That stupid woman! If only she had paid attention to me. Look at all the trouble she has made for herself. She'll be a criminal the rest of her life. Henry will be disgraced. I don't want to hear her name spoken in this house again." He jumped up and stomped out of the room.

George was dumbfounded and hurt by his Grandfather's attack on his mother. Grandmother Herzberg supported her husband, but whispered to George that she worried, because her husband seemed so angry lately. Nothing seemed to please him. He seemed angry with himself and he took his anger out on the rest of the family. At times he was so short of breath that he could hardly speak, which made him angrier still. "Often he will come in from the fields, collapse in his chair and gasp for breath. He's too stubborn to go to the doctor. Stupid old man, he doesn't see how he is disrupting the family by being so stubborn."

About a week later, Grandfather Herzberg came in from working the fields. He slumped into his chair, exhausted. He was red in the face, sweating profusely and gasping for breath. Finally he roused himself and called out for someone to bring him a glass of *schnaps*. When no one came he staggered to his feet, then collapsed on the floor. When Grandmother came into the room with his *schnaps*, she found him lying on the floor. She immediately called the doctor, but by the time he came, Grandfather Herzberg was dead. It was a shock to everyone. George sent a telegram to his mother. Anna telegraphed back saying that she was unable to come because the FBI still held her passport, but Henry would come.

This delighted George, for he hadn't seen his brother in nearly eight years. Two weeks later, Henry stepped off the train to be greeted joyfully by his brother. People looked twice as the twins walked down the platform, sure they were seeing double. Henry was a little thinner.

The gloom on the farm depressed Henry. At dinner, Grandmother sat at the head of the dining room table, fully arrayed in her widow's weeds. His two pale aunts, with haunted eyes, also dressed in black, sat stiffly on either side of her. His uncle sat at the other end of the table, looking very solemn, but saying little. Next to him sat the round-faced Klaus in his black and silver SS uniform. Klaus glared at the twins, but said nothing. The whole conversation revolved around death. Any mention of Grandfather Herzberg brought tears to Grandmother's eyes, and unctuous platitudes from the aunts, who seemed terrified. The whole atmosphere was very gloomy and depressing.

The twins finished their meal in silence and left the table as soon as possible. They slipped out the back door and found peace under one of the large trees in the yard, where they could talk more freely. Henry couldn't see what he might do to help, and George's work with the *Abwehr* took him away from the farm. They were sitting there chatting when one of the aunts called to them saying their Grandmother wished to speak to them. Reluctantly, they went into the house. In the library, Grandmother was seated in Grandfather's big chair. In one corner of the room was the Nazi flag, and over the fireplace hung a framed portrait of Hitler. As soon as the twins came in, Grandmother launched into a diatribe against Anna, her unfaithful daughter. She blamed Anna for not coming to her father's funeral. It showed great disrespect for the family.

She turned to the twins. "You, George and Henry, now have all the responsibility of the family honor to uphold. Henry, I expect you to stay here and help run the farm. Your uncle is far too busy with his own estate. Klaus is following a noble profession in the Gestapo. George, you have your government work to do, so you won't be much help. Henry, I expect you to start tomorrow."

Henry was taken aback, but replied in a quiet voice, saying that he had no intention of staying on the farm. He wasn't interested in his Grandfather's estate. His life was in Ohio with his mother.

Grandmother scowled and yelled at him. "It is your duty as a good German to continue your Grandfather's great work. It is your duty to support the *Fuhrer* and the Party, and to make Germany the most powerful country in the world. Never mind that fickle mother of yours."

"Sorry, Grandmother, to disappoint you, but I don't like farming and I don't agree with the Party."

These were brave words. Grandmother glared and screamed at her impudent grandson. Then, throwing her shawl over her head, she rocked back and forth and moaned. The twins got up and left the library, slipping past the pale aunts, who were sitting just outside the door. One of them whispered to the twins that they should make arrangements for Henry to leave as soon as possible. The aunts feared their mother's wrath, but they hurried into the library to see what they could do. Grandmother was screaming that she would send the police after Henry.

Henry was now in grave danger. Neither of the twins knew what their grandmother might do, so that night they left the farm quietly and headed for Berlin, saying goodbye to the aunts only. It was obvious that Henry had to leave the country as quickly as possible.

When they arrived in Berlin, they went directly to George's boarding house. The next morning, George went off to the *Abwehr* office and Henry walked across the street to the zoo. He watched the ducks and geese swim lazily around the lake. There were a few birds singing, but mainly it was quiet and quite peaceful.

Suddenly the silence was broken by the scream of sirens. Gestapo and police cars raced down the street and turned into a lane. Henry could hear shrieks of terror, cries of pain, and the thud of night sticks. Then he saw the beaten, bloody men hustled into waiting vans to be taken to Gestapo headquarters and almost certain death. The rest, mostly women and children, lay wounded and bleeding in the street. Another corps of SS herded them into trucks for deportation. One passerby nodded and said, "Good riddance! The Jews cause nothing but trouble. Germany will be a better place without them!" Other pedestrians just hurried on their way, saying nothing. The whole incident shocked and depressed Henry. Was there no compassion for these poor people?

The Admiral was very pleased to see George. "There is going to be a war either this spring or in the fall," he said. "The *Fuhrer* has decided, and I am worried. We can only hope his plans are successful, that it will bring a victory and we will not be involved in a two-front war. We are still not prepared for a major offensive."

"Sir," George said, his voice sounding urgent. "I have a problem. My brother, Henry, is here, but he has to get out of the country fast. Grandmother Herzberg ordered him to stay and work the farm, but he refused and told her that he didn't agree with her or the Party. She is furious, and we don't know what she might do. What do you suggest?"

The Admiral thought for a moment before he replied. "Your brother is a brave man, and I want to meet him. Bring him to the office after lunch. I may have some suggestions."

George found Henry admiring the birds in the zoo. They walked beside the lake, stopping at a sausage stand to buy lunch, which they ate sitting on a nearby bench. Henry told him about the Gestapo sweep and the remarks he'd heard. When they'd finished lunch, they walked toward the OKW Building. There was military activity around the front door. The street was full of uniformed, high-ranking army officers, so George led Henry around the back of the building and in by the rear door. They slipped up the back stairs and knocked on an unmarked door.

The Admiral was waiting. He looked at the two young men—at one then the other, and back again. He shook his head. "If I didn't know better, I couldn't tell you apart. Your grandmother has alerted the police and she wants Henry back on the farm. We know that is impossible, but now both of you are in danger. I can't afford to lose George; he is too valuable to the *Abwehr*. But I can help get Henry out of the country." He looked at

Henry. "Thank goodness you have an American passport. You can't go into France, because George is a marked man. Belgium is being very stuffy and stiff-necked about people coming from Germany." The Admiral glanced at the map of Europe on the wall behind him. "However, I do know an obscure crossing into Luxembourg. I have used it myself upon occasion. Henry, give me your passport and I will get you an exit visa."

Henry surrendered his passport with some reluctance. The Admiral reached into his briefcase lying on the table, and produced identification cards with all the proper stamps and seals. Then he dismissed them, telling them to come back the next afternoon.

They returned to George's boarding house and told the landlady that they would be going away for a few days. In the morning, they walked through the Tiergarten, lunched at the boarding house, packed their gear and went to the *Abwehr* office. The Admiral was waiting.

"Here are your orders. The car is in the back lot, and all the orders, permits, maps, and identification are here in this packet. There is even a little money." He handed them a thick brown envelope. "You are on official *Abwehr* business. George, you will drive Henry to the Vianden crossing. I'll see you back here in a week, for we have serious work to do. Henry, change out of your uniform before you reach the crossing. Once you have crossed the border, head for Rotterdam. I think you can catch a ship there. Remember, if the police stop you, tell them you are with *Abwehr*. I'm very glad to have met you, good luck on your trip home, and may God bless you." The Admiral shook hands with the twins and left the room. George and Henry changed into rather plain-looking *Abwehr* uniforms and went down the back stairs to the car.

The trip to Halle was uneventful. They saw the usual display of uniforms of all ranks. From Halle they drove to Koblenz on the Rhine. They pulled up in front of a small pension on a side street. After inspecting their papers, the landlady welcomed them for supper and the night. She said she was always glad to take in any officers of the Reich. It was only the ugly foreigners and Jews that she couldn't abide.

George and Henry left the next morning. Although the landlady had been pleasant, they suspected that she had reported them to the local police. Ten kilometers outside Koblenz, on the road to Trier, there was a police roadblock. George produced their *Abwehr* cards and orders, and became quite arrogant. Why were they delaying officers of the *Abwehr*? The police said they had orders to arrest a Heinrich Hill. George said it was obvious that neither of them were Heinrich Hill. The police apologized, saluted and waved them on.

Henry had to get out of country fast. At Trier they turned north along the valley of the Our River. The road wound through some lovely rolling farmland. They stopped at the crest of a hill. Below them was the little stone bridge marking the boundary between Germany and Luxembourg. Henry changed his clothes, leaving the *Abwehr* uniform in the car. They dropped down to the river. They embraced, for they didn't know when they would see each other again. Henry presented his American passport and exit visa to German border guards and they waved him through. In the middle of the bridge he turned and waved. George waved back and turned away. He hated to see his brother go. There were tears in Henry's eyes as crossed the bridge. He, too, hated to leave his brother. He cleared the Luxembourg customs easily and looked back across the river, but George had gone. With a heavy heart he walked into town.

George drove back to Koblenz, but this time he stayed at a different pension. In the morning, just before crossing the bridge over the Rhine, there was another police roadblock. They showed him a picture of Henry. George insisted he was Géorg Berg of the *Abwehr* and knew nothing of this Heinrich Hill. There might be some resemblance, but he didn't know him. If they didn't believe him they could call the *Abwehr* office in Berlin. *Thank goodness*, he thought. *Henry is out of the country.* The police didn't want to take a chance with the *Abwehr*, so they let him cross the bridge. It was close, too close.

He arrived back in Berlin and reported to the Admiral. When he mentioned the two roadblocks, the Admiral raised his eyebrows and said, "It was close, but I'm glad Henry made it. He may have a few problems, but he'll get home all right. George, you report back here tomorrow, for we have things to discuss. The *Fubrer* has ordered the High Command to prepare to march on Czechoslovakia. Those overstuffed generals downstairs are delighted. A major war is not far away, and we are still not fully prepared." He shook is head sadly and dismissed George.

After George left, the Admiral took out a folder and studied it for a long time. There were gaps in his intelligence. There were things he needed to know. He would send George on another mission: first to find out the conditions in Belgium, and second to get him out of the country for awhile. He didn't want this fuss with Grandmother Herzberg to interfere with his plans. He knew that Hitler planned to invade Poland. After that, Hitler most certainly would turn his attention to the West. The Admiral and a few others of the general staff knew that Germany was not prepared for war and could not win a major war, no matter how much boasting the *Fuhrer* and the Party engaged in. As much as the Admiral and his friends disliked Hitler and the Party, orders were orders, and you obeyed.

8

Henry

ENRY SHOULDERED HIS BACKPACK and walked slowly into the small village of Vianden. He checked into the local hotel. He hated to leave George, and he worried about him. That night he wrote him a long letter, saying he would probably be back in Barnesville within a month. In the morning, he inquired as to the best way to get to Liege and Maastricht, and they told him to take the bus to Luxembourg City, then take the train north. He left on the bus within the hour.

In the city, the newspapers were all proclaiming that the Godesberg conference between Hitler and Chamberlain, and the other international conferences, ensured peace in Europe for the next ten years. Hitler had stated that Germany wanted no further territory, and all the western nations believed him. This made Henry very sad, for he had seen the other side and knew that Germany was preparing for war. He didn't trust Hitler or the Party. He had seen the ugly, terrifying campaigns against the Jews and other so-called "undesirables." He has also seen the atrocious lies the Nazi government paraded as truth. That night, while having dinner in Luxembourg he mentioned these things, but nobody else agreed with him. He was wrong, they said, for everybody knew the wonders Hitler had wrought for Germany. He had brought law, order, stability and peace to Europe.

The next morning, Henry caught the train north. He shared a compartment with an old Belgian couple, and a pair of young German hikers. They soon got into a heated discussion about the possibility of war. The old couple had experienced the Great War and all the horrors of the German invasion and occupation of Belgium. They hoped that this would not happen again. This was all quite unknown to the young hikers; they saw only the glory in Hitler's promises. Henry did his best to keep quiet, but they wanted to know his opinion.

When the train squealed to a stop at the Belgian frontier, the border guards checked passports and travel papers. A customs official asked Henry to state his destination, and he replied Rotterdam. The border guard nodded and said there would be a two-hour wait in Liege, but he was not to leave the station. Belgium had mobilized its army, and there were uniforms everywhere. King Leopold III had proclaimed Belgium's strict neutrality and had canceled its treaties with France and Britain.

Henry walked up and down the Liege station platform. He bought a cup of insipid coffee and a croissant. The headlines in the local newspaper praised the King for his forceful action. As Henry boarded the train he thought *What an empty gesture! Germany will ignore Belgium's neutrality, treaty or no treaty.* The railway carriage was now occupied by a Dutch family returning home, and the young Germans. The whistle blew, the train started with a lurch, and headed north to Maastricht. They crossed the Dutch border within an hour. Again questions of destination, and again nods of acceptance. The two young Germans were not so lucky. The border guards took them off the train for questioning. Henry got off the train in Maastricht. It had been a tiring day. He registered at the hotel across the street from the station. After a good dinner and a warm bath he felt relaxed, and began to reflect on the dire circumstances that surrounded him. Although the train trip on the morrow would be relatively easy and should get him to Rotterdam in good time, George was returning to work for the military intelligence. Notwithstanding the protective hand of the Admiral, George was, after all, part of the German military machine. The Admiral had hinted broadly that war might break out at any time. The great fear, from the Admiral's point of view, was not knowing how France or Britain would react. All these thoughts Henry wrote in his journal. Sitting there, he felt very alone, and very far from home. He wrote a letter to his mother telling her all that had happened. He realized that he no longer had to look over his shoulder, or watch what he said. The feeling of freedom of speech and thought was exhilarating—in contrast to Germany, where speech and actions were so controlled. He wondered how George endured the strain.

The next day, he arrived in Rotterdam only to find that there were no scheduled Atlantic sailings. The American Consul advised him to get to Britain and sail from there. He hitched a ride with a truck to the Hoek van Holland, but the Dutch customs agent wouldn't let him sail because he did not have an appropriate visa. Much to his disgust he caught the last tram back to Rotterdam.

Henry spent a frustrating morning in the British consulate. The consular agents were very suspicious. Why did he want to go to Britain? Would he being staying any length of time in the country? Did he know anybody in Britain? Where had he been? Why had he been he in Germany? He faced a barrage of similar, utterly stupid questions.

Henry did his best to remain calm and answer the questions as honestly as he could. To him it was so obvious: he just wanted to sail for home. The consul took his application and told him to come back in two days. They said they had to wire London for authorization to issue a visa. Discouraged, he left the consulate and walked along the docks. A small Dutch freighter, the *Haarlam*, was tied up to the dock. The first officer was leaning on the rail. He called down to Henry, and asked him if he wanted a job. Henry looked up, then walked up the gangplank.

The *Haarlam* was due to sail later that afternoon. Its destinations were Halifax, south Florida, and then Dutch Antilles. They needed extra deck hands for the two-week Atlantic run. Henry could work for his passage to Halifax and, depending on how he did, there may be a bonus. Entering Canada would be no problem. Henry was anxious to get home, and his money was running low. While they were discussing terms, the captain walked over to them—a stocky seafaring Dutchman with startling blues eyes. He listened, nodded, and then extended his hand to welcome Henry on board.

The *Haarlam* slipped out of Rotterdam at high tide, and sailed right into a howling, north-sea gale. The channel was rough and the waves high. The *Haarlam* bucked and heaved from one crest to the next. Laboriously she made her way south along the coast. The wind howled through the rigging, and wild waves crashed down on the deck. There was concern whether the *Haarlam* could stand the continuous pounding. By nightfall, the wind has increased and screamed like a maniac; in the morning it dropped to a howl. But the waves still pounded the ship.

During the night, some of the deck plates had sprung their rivets. In the light of day, it was obvious the *Haarlam* would have to head into port for repairs. Slowly she beat her way across the channel, past the Isle of Wight and into the dockyards at Portsmouth. The damage was more extensive than first realized, and the repairs would involve at least a week's delay. Henry had no visa to land in Britain, so he acted as watchman. He wrote to his mother, hoping that his letter would get to Ohio before he did, and also wrote a long letter to George. He mailed the letters and was standing on the dock watching the sunset. A British staff officer came by and stopped.

"What are you doing here?"

"Just watching the sunset."

"I saw you in London two days ago."

"No, I've been here all week."

"I'm sure it was you. Weren't you in the Savoy lounge?"

"Sorry, it was not I. I've never been to London."

"He certainly looked like you."

Henry knew that the officer had seen George, but he wasn't about to say anything. The staff officer doubted Henry's denial. "You better be gone tomorrow or I'll have you in for questioning."

Henry turned quickly and went up the gangplank. He wanted no more of that.

• • •

With repairs completed, and the fuel and water tanks topped up, the *Haarlam* set sail again. The Channel waves were still angry, but nothing really serious. They sailed around the coast of Ireland and headed for the open sea. In the first days the grey, greasy swells of the North Atlantic slowed their progress, so they put in to Reykjavík for provisioning. The captain radioed the company for instructions. Head office felt they had lost too much time already, and ordered the *Haarlam* to bypass Halifax and Florida, and sail directly to the Antilles. The captain called Henry to the wardroom and advised him of these new orders. Henry had the choice of staying in Iceland or continuing to the Antilles. The captain told him he would have to make up his mind within 24 hours.

Henry was still far from home, and this was disheartening news. He walked over to the Harbormaster's office to check on other sailings. Harbormaster, Lars Pederson, was very understanding. If Henry didn't mind sailing on a fishing boat, there was one due to sail for St. John's, Newfoundland, in a day or two, and they were looking for extra hands. Henry returned to the *Haarlam*, picked up his gear and his pay, thanked the captain and went ashore.

Lars invited Henry to stay at his place for the night. At the end of the day, they walked through the town to the Pederson home, a neat, colorful house with a bright blue door, and set in a small garden full of flowers.

As they walked up the path, the blue door swung open and Henry was welcomed in warm Icelandic fashion. There were five at supper, Lars, his wife, Katherine, and their two beautiful daughters, Kajsa, eighteen, and Marguerite, twenty. They all wanted to know of his adventures and why he was in Iceland. Their supper was a table of good food and a time of excellent conversation.

They were most interested to hear about George and Germany, but Henry could barely keep his mind on the topics. His eyes kept returning to the beautiful Marguerite. The harbormaster's wife was quick to notice the looks and smiles that went back and forth between the two. After supper, she suggested that Marguerite show Henry the town. They walked out together, blushing and feeling a little shy, but it wasn't long before they were talking freely. Henry had fallen in love with Marguerite and she with him.

The next day, Marguerite packed a picnic for two. They walked out of town along the coast toward the hot springs, to a secluded little cove out of the wind. Not much of the picnic lunch was eaten, as they only wanted to lie in each other's arms and pledge their love. Late in the afternoon they strolled back, talking and holding hands. They told Marguerite's parents that they were very much in love and wanted get married. Lars and Katherine listened, smiled, and yes, they would agree, but first Henry had to return to Ohio and tell his mother. Then he could come back to Iceland and marry Marguerite. Little did either of them know the curves, the detours, and the bumps that lay ahead. They only knew they had fallen in love.

When the fishing trawler departed, Marguerite stood on the dock and watched her love sail away. Would she ever see him again? She walked home with tears in her eyes. Henry stood on the deck until the dock was out of sight. He was leaving his new-found love with a very heavy heart. Three days of uneventful sailing brought them into St. John's harbor. He cleared Newfoundland customs and immigration quite easily. That night, in the mariner's hostel, he wrote a long, passionate letter to Marguerite.

9

Berlin

IT WAS A BEAUTIFUL DAY, A RARITY IN BERLIN. On that morning George walked from his lodgings to the *OKW* Building. There was no bustle this time, just a few sleepy guards in the lobby. He made his way upstairs to the *Abwehr* office and knocked on the door. When he entered, the Admiral got up and put on his greatcoat and cap. He beckoned George to follow him.

They walked past the burned-out shell of the old *Reichstag* building into the *Tiergarten*, and sat down on a bench overlooking the River Spree. The Admiral had said nothing to this point, but now he began speak in a low voice.

"The General Staff knows that Germany is not prepared for an all-out war. They have a plan to replace Hitler if there is such a war. Therefore, the General Staff is sending Ewald von Kliest, as their representative to London, to seek an agreement with the British government that they will stand firm with Czechoslovakia. Their purpose is to prevent further German aggression, as such action will cause widespread conflict across Europe. The generals would then overthrow Hitler and negotiate a peace treaty." The Admiral paused and looked at George.

"I want you to go as the aide to Ewald von Kliest. His English is poor, and the generals need to know the British position in order to carry out their plans to replace Hitler. If the British fail to agree, Hitler will be stronger and more arrogant than ever. Sooner or later, there will be another war, like the Great War of 1914–18, and we are not prepared to fight the

51

combined forces of France, Britain, and possibly the Soviet Union. Hitler feels if he can defeat France, then Great Britain will surrender. Then together they can attack and defeat the Soviet Union. He is convinced that the Russian people will rise in support of the German Army and overthrow the Soviet government. It is madness, and I am deeply pessimistic about the outcome. You will leave with Ewald von Kliest tomorrow. He will be in London for a week, meeting with British officials. When you return, report back to me." He left George with instructions to buy a new suit for the trip.

George and Ewald von Kliest flew to London the next day. There were interviews with Churchill, but none officially with the government; only a minor foreign office official talked to them. Prime Minister Chamberlain's government would not even talk to them, and dismissed the whole mission as foolish and of no consequence. The British government continued to follow blindly their policy of promoting European peace through appeasement, no matter what the cost.

All things considered, George had a good time in London. He spent a delightful evening in the Savoy Lounge, discussing the whole European situation with a British junior staff officer who thought George was an American. He spent another equally delightful evening at the theater in the company of the charming Ann Catchpool, whom he had met in the officers' club. She, too, thought he was an American.

The mission was a failure. In refusing to meet with the representative of the German General Staff, Neville Chamberlain, had unwittingly given Hitler a reprieve. There would be no palace revolution of the generals now. George returned to Berlin to find the Admiral in a very gloomy mood, afraid that Hitler, so encouraged by his bloodless victories, would try something rash.

"George, I want you to go to Belgium. King Leopold III has declared his neutrality, but we don't know how solid that is. We feel fairly sure of what France and Britain will do in the face of some new aggression by Hitler. They will do nothing! What I need to know is Belgium's true position. Will they join France and Britain in the case of war, or will they try to maintain their neutrality? The young King is so unpredictable.

"Travel around the country, talk to people. Check on the fortifications and security measures, particularly along the border. All this information is of vital importance, because Hitler is planning to attack the West. Take your time—you'll need a month or so."

The Admiral was worried, as the invasion of Czechoslovakia was imminent. He wasn't sure if this meant war or not. He hoped not. He was very fond of George, and his talents, and he wanted to get him out of the country in case there was war. This trip to Belgium was necessary, for there was not enough known about their defenses. Supposedly, they had a great line of fortifications along the River Maas, but exactly how strong they were was up to George to discover?

The Admiral attended a secret conference with the stuffy generals and the *Fuhrer*. The *Fuhrer* announced that the invasion of Czechoslovakia would take place, as planned, within the next two weeks. Then the *Fuhrer* said, "Czechoslovakia will be no more; Poland will be next. The invasion of Poland is to begin September 1. If there is to be a war with Britain and France, then the Reich will need Poland's agriculture to supply food for the Reich." By the end of summer, the *Fuhrer* wanted a detailed report from the Admiral on the defenses of the low countries, particularly their coastal air bases.

George was glad to get out of Germany. The restrictions of the government were burdensome, and Party control was ever more oppressive. The Gestapo-SS was seizing power wherever they could. George hated being a Nazi, but if he was to survive, he had to be.

The next day, he took the train for Aachen. In the compartment with him were some American tourists and a ranking German officer. The young Americans were impressed with the orderliness of Germany. The army officer, wanting to practice his English, explained the Nazi philosophy of racial purity to them. He asked them why the Americans hated Germany so much. The tourists said that wasn't so, they admired Germany and felt Hitler had accomplished great things. It all sounded so reasonable. George just listened, pretending not to understand. He was saddened by the naïveté of the Americans and the narrowness and gullibility of the German officer. As the train rolled through the countryside he thought of Henry and wondered what he would do in this situation. He envied Henry and wished he could be in Ohio. Maybe, someday, when this frightful mess was over, he too would enjoy freedom.

The train stopped in Aachen for a border check. The army officer saluted the two Americans and got off the train. Two SS border guards in black uniforms came through the car checking passports and travel documents. George's *Abwehr* passport was enough to let him continue. The young Americans were detained for questioning. A few miles further, the Belgian patrols came through. This time, George had a valid American passport, and proper travel papers. The train continued to Liege. George checked into the best hotel in town. After dinner, he read Henry's most recent letter again and then wrote him a long letter in return, expressing his fears that war was on the horizon. He felt that both France and Great Britain were blind to the dangers that lay ahead. Here in Belgium, he didn't have to write to his brother in code.

The next day George went shopping for some good hiking clothes and equipment—a knapsack, boots, camera, and a pair of excellent binoculars—all paid for with American dollars. He was the epitome of the well-dressed American outdoorsman—his cover persona. He hiked and camped throughout the Ardennes, observing and taking notes on the wildlife and birds. This was the French-speaking area of Belgium, a heavily forested area interlaced with woodland trails and narrow roads. The forest bordered Luxembourg on the south and extended well into France on the west. He took pictures, made notes, and drew sketch maps of the eastern part of the forest. He talked to the local peasants, who often invited him in for a meal or to stay overnight. Many had experienced the devastation of the Great War, and were still bitter in their condemnation of the German Army. But at the same time there was a begrudging admiration of Hitler. After all, they said, "He did bring Germany out of the depression."

In this area, the depression had caused severe distress through a lowering of farm prices and a decline in the value of the franc. The peasants felt that the government in Brussels didn't care about them. George often heard Belgians say, "It's those penny-pinching Flemish who cause all this trouble. It's too bad the young king listens to them all the time."

George caught the bus back to Liege and checked into the hotel. He was ready for a hot bath and a good meal. He noticed the headline in the local newspaper: "German Army Invades Czechoslovakia Without Opposition." According to German sources, the Czechs had asked for protection, as had the Austrians. George didn't believe that. He was sure that the Czech government had been pressured and hounded into agreeing. It had been one of the aims of the *Fuhrer*, as stated in *Mein Kampf*, to destroy the Czechs. The Waffen-SS, under the command of Heinrich Himmler, and the Gestapo, commanded by Reinhard Heydrich, were now in full control of the country. Slovakia, led by Father Tiso, remained semi-independent. One more country had fallen victim to German tyranny and its relentless march eastward. It was obvious to George that Poland would be next. The Belgian newspapers praised Hitler for avoiding a war. With that trouble spot out of the way, maybe there would be stability and peace in Europe. They ignored the fact that Hitler had solemnly promised, following the Munich conference, that Germany had no further territorial ambitions. It depressed George to think that there was so little understanding of National Socialism and Hitler. Countries like Belgium seemed so eager to accept the German propaganda.

The next day he took the train to Gent. He checked into a four-star hotel, submitting his American passport for police inspection. All was in order, so he was free to travel around as he wished. After a day of shopping in Gent he took the bus to Brugge. This old city served as his base, as he wandered the coastal areas of Flanders. This time he posed as an American birdwatcher searching for rare seabirds. The Flemish farmers were very helpful, pointing out the most likely areas. The Belgian defenses in the west were woeful. There were few air bases, most of them in disrepair. Scars of the Great War could still be seen.

He spent a delightful, warm, sunny weekend in the seaside town of Oostende. He found this to be an ideal setting for writing his final report. He also wrote a letter to Henry, commenting on the attitudes of the Belgians. The general feeling of the local Flemish population was that the young king would keep them out of war. They blamed the French-speaking Walhoons for urging Belgium to stand with France.

The train trip back to Berlin was uneventful. George realized that sooner or later he would have to leave Germany. He had a good job with the military intelligence under the protection of the Admiral, but supersensitive spying was beginning to worry him. Upon arrival, he went to see the Admiral and handed in his final report. The Admiral was very pleased. After a few days break in Berlin, the balance of George's summer was taken up with a variety of much shorter, but similarly important missions on behalf of the *Abwehr*.

Late in August the Admiral called him into his office. He beckoned George to follow him to a car waiting at the curb. They climbed in and were driven out to San Sousi, the Rococo palace of Frederick II of Prussia at Potsdam. It was a smaller version of the Great Palace at Versailles.

When they arrived, the Admiral dismissed the driver. He and George walked through the beautiful grounds and sat on a bench overlooking a little lake. This day, Admiral Canaris looked particularly sad. His pale face was lined, and there were dark circles under his eyes. He began to talk quietly, almost musing to himself.

"George, next week marks the beginning of the end of the Reich. The Army has orders to march into Poland on September 1, and the Polish army will be crushed. Poland, as a state, will cease to exist. Our treaty with the Soviet Union will prevent their interference, we think. France and Great Britain will reluctantly declare war, yet Germany is still not prepared. But tell *that* to the pompous generals and the *Fuhrer*, and you'd be accused of treason. Even to think such thoughts is treasonous.

"You are young and have a full life ahead of you. We'll have find a way to get you out of Germany before it's too late. It will have to be done legitimately, for the spies of the SS and the Party are everywhere. As for today, we have simply enjoyed a quiet walk in the park. Go back to the family farm for a visit, for it may be the last chance you'll have."

George left Berlin with a most uneasy feeling. The Admiral was confiding in him, but he wasn't quite sure what it all meant. He would have to be very careful, and say nothing.

He went back to the farm to visit his grandmother and the pale aunts. Grandmother Herzberg still hadn't forgiven Henry for running away, but she was sure that George had nothing to do with it. The papers accused the vicious Poles of invading the Fatherland and blowing up a radio transmitter. In retaliation, the Army, on the *Fuhrer's* orders, had invaded Poland to stamp out terrorism. At the supper table that night Grandmother, still dressed in black, extolled the glories of the Reich and praised George for his role in the military.

"Germany has to defend herself," she said, waving a finger in defiance. "Isn't it wonderful that we have the *Fuhrer* to lead Germany back to her proper place in the world? Now England and France will take notice. How stupid for Henry and that mother of his to live in that decadent, Jew-dominated country, when they could have enjoyed peace and harmony here in the Fatherland."

The pale aunts said nothing, but they looked sad. Grandmother's limited vision depressed George. Ever since Henry's break with their grandmother, George felt that he did not belong in the family. He had a good relationship with his aunts, with whom he enjoyed talking, but because they feared their mother so much, their conversation at the dinner table was limited. That night he excused himself from the table just as soon as it was polite to do so and went upstairs to his room. He wrote a letter to Henry, expressing his and the Admiral's views on the situation. He missed Henry and wondered what he was doing.

George tarried a few days more, then took the train back to Berlin. The train overflowed with the different-colored uniforms of the various services. Those in civilian dress were in the minority and thus attracted the most attention. George's simple gray army uniform allowed him to avoid scrutiny. Back in Berlin, the main floor of the OKW Building was crowded with officers, so George went in by the back door and up the back stairs.

The Admiral welcomed him but launched into detailed explanation before they were seated. "Great Britain and France have declared war on Germany today. Belgium has proclaimed its neutrality. Now begins the death struggle, and Germany cannot win. The *Fuhrer* is mad with power. He will blame all of Germany's troubles on the Jews, the Communists, and anybody in opposition. He means to exterminate every Jew in

Germany. Many concentration camps, now under the control of the SS already have gas chambers and crematoriums in full operation. There are a few of us who are very afraid. But orders, as you know, are orders, and we will do our best, even if it means our death and the total destruction of Germany." With a wave of his hand he dismissed George.

George walked along the Spree. Geese and swans were swimming peacefully among the reeds. He envied them, for he yearned for a life of peace, and he had no idea where his next assignment might take him. He thought of his mother and Henry, and felt very lonely and sad.

10

Homeward Bound

HENRY HAD DISEMBARKED IN ST. JOHN'S, but he was still a long way from home. He cleared Newfoundland customs by answering the usual stupid questions, then shouldered his backpack and walked up the hill to the mariner's hostel where he would stay overnight. This morning, he made his way to the train station. The train, locally known as *Newfie Bullet* for its lack of speed, was standing in the station. The polished engine puffed quietly to itself. Coupled behind was a baggage car and three coaches, painted in pink, white and green. The schedule said the trip to Channel-Port aux Basques on the west coast took eight hours, but one never knew. The conductor was sweeping out the coach vestibule as Henry approached.

"Ah, you're traveling with us this day."

"Yes," Henry said.

"Ah, 'tis a beautiful, blessed day."

Henry stepped in and took a seat among the few passengers in the third coach. Suddenly there was a commotion on the platform, and a farmer appeared driving a large hog. After the hog had been stowed in the baggage car, the farmer, red-faced and winded, joined his boisterous family, who had preceded him and settled in the rear of the coach. The whistle blew and train eased out of the station. For the next twelve hours the *Bullet* made its way leisurely across Newfoundland, stopping at every small town and finally swinging down the west coast to Channel-Port aux Basques.

Henry just had time to catch the night ferry to Sydney, Nova Scotia. Tired and hungry, he managed to find an empty chair in the lounge and catch a few hours sleep. In the morning he wrote a letter to Marguerite and posted it in Sydney. George would have to wait. After a cup of coffee and a sandwich he caught a slow local train to Port Hawksbury, took another ferry trip to Mulgrave and then another slow train to Halifax, and finally, by yet another train, he got to Montreal. He skimped on food and often slept in the stations. Home still seemed to be far away in one direction and Iceland was becoming farther away in the other. At times, Henry was tempted to rush back to Marguerite, but he had promised Lars and Katherine he would go home first.

His money was almost gone. He had enough for a ticket from Montreal to Albany and, if he was careful, enough for some food. The train crossed the border at Champlain, where the customs officials were curious to know where Henry had been and why he'd come into the US that way. After lengthy explanations, they let him continue to Albany.

The US was still recovering from the depression, and unemployment remained high. Men could still be seen riding the rails looking for work. Henry walked along the tracks. He had to get to Cleveland and began watching for a freight leaving the yards heading west. Waiting in the shadow of some empty cars, he could see cars moving two or three tracks over. Falling into step with the slow-moving freight, Henry swung himself into an empty box car, and soon curled up in a dark corner and went to sleep. Later he was awakened by someone kicking him in the ribs and shining a light in his face. He opened his eyes and saw a railroad cop standing over him. The cop wanted to know where he was going. Henry stood up and stretched. "Cleveland," he said.

"You're not the usual kind of tramp we get around here, but you can't ride this freight. If you slip over two tracks you can catch another one." The cop pointed across the yard.

"Thanks, I will."

Henry jumped down, ducked under the coupling and crossed the tracks. Another westbound freight was just under way. Henry swung himself onto a flatcar. It was the middle of the night when they reached Cleveland, and he was cold and hungry. At least he was in Ohio, and only 50 miles from home!

In the end, Henry walked that 50 miles, arriving at his grandfather's farm tired, dirty, and very hungry. His clothes and shoes were in terrible shape. He walked into the kitchen, and at first his grandmother didn't recognize him, then she threw her arms around him.

"Oh, Henry, we prayed for thy safety and that thee would return home to us. Where did thee come from?"

"Oh, Grandmother, I am so glad to be home. I walked all the way from Cleveland, and what I would like most is a hot bath, some clean clothes and a decent meal."

"Thee just go right upstairs. There is plenty of hot water, and I think there are clothes of thine in the cupboard. I will call thy mother and tell her that thee is safely home."

Henry set his knapsack in the porch, took off his shoes and went upstairs. An hour later he came down, washed, shaved and wearing clean clothes. He was thin and pale, but certainly cleaner, and feeling more like his old self again. His mother, Uncle John, Emily and Grandfather were all waiting in the kitchen. Everyone's joy was unbounded.

At supper, Grandfather offered a prayer of thanksgiving for Henry's safe return. Then they had to hear the news. First and most important, Henry told of his engagement to the beautiful Marguerite. Then he told of Germany and George, and finally of his trip home. Grandfather wanted to know why he had walked from Cleveland.

"I had no money, Grandfather."

Henry went home with his mother and they talked until he fell asleep. She wanted to know about her family, Germany and, most of all, about George. He told her George would be all right, for he was under the protection of Admiral Canaris. He told her of the Admiral's help in getting him out of Germany, and of his refusal to stay and run the farm for Grandmother Herzberg.

"Oh, Mother, she was furious with me. When she realized we had left, she sent the police after us. Germany is a frightful, depressing country, a country ruled by terror and fear. The press and radio are controlled and it is dangerous to speak your mind. The Gestapo and the Party have their spies everywhere. When he couldn't keep his eyes open any longer, he kissed his mother, picked up Marguerite's and George's letters and went to bed. He would read them later.

Henry slept around the clock and, when he finally awoke, he saw a small face looking at him. It was his young stepsister, Emily, standing by his bed looking very solemn. He hugged her, and gave her a big kiss. She said, "Mother is waiting downstairs and lunch is ready."

"I'll be right there, and I'm hungry. Now run along while I dress."

The trip home had taken the best part of two months. Henry had met some wonderful helpful people along the way. Both Marguerite and George would have been very anxious to hear from him, and all about his journey and safe return to Ohio. He had a leisurely lunch with his mother and Emily, who, with solemn eyes, watched her older brother earnestly as he ate. To her, he was wonderful—and mysterious.

After lunch Henry retired to the living room and wrote a long, passionate letter to Marguerite and then an equally long letter to George, telling him particularly of his encounter with the British officer in Portsmouth. In both, he told of his adventures and difficulties in getting home. He told George that he could never explain America to Grandmother Herzberg, nor could he completely understand the narrowness of the German point of view. Anna wrote a long loving letter to Marguerite welcoming her to the family.

The next few weeks were frustrating. Henry could find no transportation to return to Iceland. The shipping lines had curtailed their sailings for fear of war. Freighters for Europe didn't stop at Iceland. There were a few fishing boats from Newfoundland, but these were irregular and uncertain. By the time war in Europe started, all transportation to Iceland had ceased. Even American freighters, though technically neutral, were stopped and searched by the German U-boats. It was equally frustrating for Marguerite, for she longed to be with Henry, who had to content himself by working on Grandfather Hill's farm.

Two letters came from George, in English, telling of his travels in Belgium. Although he couldn't be specific about his mission, Henry was able to read between the lines. George expressed his fears of an all-out war in Europe and what the consequences might be.

Late in the summer of the same year Henry managed to get passage on a freighter sailing from Halifax for Reykjavík with a cargo of supplies. It would return two weeks hence with a load of fish. Henry arrived in Halifax and found the small freighter, the *Julia B*, tied up ready to sail. He boarded and checked in with the first mate. That night they slipped out of the harbor on the tide. The summer had been particularly warm, so there were more icebergs than usual. This forced the *Julia B* to swing far south of her usual course. A cold wind blew down from Davis Inlet, pushing the giant icebergs ahead of it. These great towering structures of ice floated majestically toward warmer water. The *Julia B* had to be on constant lookout for these giants.

The freighter pulled into Reykjavík harbor three days late. Marguerite, bundled up in a greatcoat, stood on the dock. She had been on the dock every day anxiously awaiting the arrival of the *Julia B* and her true love. Henry was first down the gangplank, and they fell into each others arms. Great was the joy in the Pederson house that evening. Katherine had a special dinner for friends and family. In the morning they all sat around the breakfast table and made plans for Marguerite and Henry's wedding. They had very few days in which to do so before the freighter was due to sail again. Katherine sent Henry and Marguerite to the registry office for a marriage license, and then on to the church to consult with the pastor. Katherine and Kajsa were busy with preparations for the wedding breakfast and reception.

Henry and Marguerite walked around town holding hands, rejoicing in each other's company. The lovebirds were oblivious to what was going on around them. Father Lars popped out of his office and called to them. "Germany has invaded Poland, and the UK and France have declared war. We don't know how this will affect Iceland, or the United States, or how long it will last."

A little later the office door slammed open and the captain of the *Julia B* came in. "Lars, I want to sail in three days. There is a big storm brewing over Greenland, and I want to be well out to sea before it strikes. Also I don't know what those damned Germans are going to do. They may have subs at sea already."

Despite the little time in which they had to prepare, the wedding was a great success, as the whole neighborhood turned out to cheer the happy couple. Family, friends and neighbors threw confetti and rice as Henry and Marguerite walked down the main street to the docks. The *Julia B*, decked out with full bunting, welcomed them aboard. The captain had even turned his cabin into a honeymoon suite for the them. Henry and Marguerite stood at the rail and, as the ship sailed out of the harbor, there was a good deal of waving from the ship to the dock and back.

Marguerite, with tears in her eyes, wondered what her life would be like now. She had never left home before, and now she didn't know when she would see Iceland again. She only knew that she was blissfully happy with Henry. She also knew that there would be a warm welcome in Ohio. She turned and buried her head in Henry's chest, and wept quietly. He held her very tenderly and stroked her hair. They stood at the rail long after they lost sight of the town, each thinking thoughts that rested firmly on the love they shared.

Two days out, a German sub surfaced and commanded them to stop. The *Julia B* was a neutral ship, flying the flag of Iceland. The young German captain, leading the boarding party, was speaking to the ship's captain when Henry and Marguerite came around the corner. When he saw Henry he clicked his heals and saluted.

"Heil Hitler! I was unaware you were aboard, sir."

Oh my God, thought Henry, *he thinks I am George, and I had better be careful.* Henry put his finger to his lips, and answered in German that he was on a top secret mission for the *Abwehr*, and that nothing was to stand in their way. "You haven't seen me. You know nothing about this. Nothing is to be reported. Is that clear?"

"Ja," the German replied, saluting again. He indicated that they would provide a hidden escort to The *Julia B* the rest of the way. After the boarding party had left, Marguerite and the captain asked what this was all about. Henry told them that his twin brother worked for the *Abwehr* and this was a case of mistaken identity. He hoped that he had pulled off the ruse. The next day, the storm struck. For two days The *Julia B* wallowed through high seas and shrieking winds, and at last limped into Halifax.

With many thanks to the captain and crew for their kindness, Henry and Marguerite left the ship. Their baggage was taken over to Pier 21—the Canadian immigration centre—to clear customs and immigration. The Canadians were most cordial and helpful. They inspected their baggage, marriage license and passports, then issued transit visas. The Canadian authorities wanted to know if they had encountered any German submarines. George explained that indeed they had encountered a German U-boat, which had been lying in wait about two days out of port. This was bad news for shipping. With their baggage cleared, they took the train for Montreal, then to Plattsburg, NY. The Americans were polite but curious. The officials asked many questions regarding Germany, the war, and Great Britain. Many of their questions Henry couldn't answer. They inspected everything again, finally allowing Henry and Marguerite to continue their journey.

The newlyweds stayed the night in New York. Marguerite had never seen such a big city. The next day they went to Penn Station and caught *The Jeffersonian* for home. The train sped across Pennsylvania, arriving at Barnesville behind schedule.

John, Anna, and Emily were waiting for the train to pull in. Anna warmly embraced her new daughter-in-law and welcomed her to Ohio. Marguerite felt a little lonely so far from home. As she stood on the platform looking around, she wondered what her new life would be like. Henry was talking to his mother and John. When Marguerite felt a small hand take hers, she looked down and saw Emily smiling up at her. That smile seemed to say *I love you and I hope you will love me too*. Marguerite bent down and hugged the young girl. Then together they walked, hand in hand, down the platform.

11

Ohio and the War

JOHN AND ANNA PACED UP AND DOWN THE PLATFORM while Emily sat on the baggage wagon swinging her feet. All were waiting for the train. Anna couldn't help wondering what her new daughter-in-law would be like, and how she would adjust to them, and they to her. *The Jeffersonian* was late, but at last it pulled into the station in a cloud of steam. Henry and Marguerite stepped onto the platform feeling a little shy. Anna rushed up and embraced Marguerite and then Henry. Henry shook hands with John and lifted the solemn-eyed Emily into the air. They loaded the baggage into the station wagon and drove out to the farm. Anna wanted to hear all the news. Had they heard anything from George? Henry related the case of mistaken identity and the presence of German submarines off the coast of Canada.

That night they had a wonderful reunion dinner at the Hill's farm. Marguerite was a little overwhelmed and overcome by the warm embrace and love from the Hill family. She felt quite at home. That night she wrote a long, loving letter to her parents before snuggling into bed and falling asleep in her beloved husband's arms.

Morning sunlight was streaming through the windows when there was a knock on the door. Henry sat up. The door opened a crack and Emily's solemn face appeared. "Mother says that breakfast is ready," she said, then smiled and retreated down the stairs. As Henry and Marguerite got dressed, they talked about moving into their own house. The smell of fresh coffee filled the room and drew them down to the kitchen. Anna was busy at the stove. Emily sat at the table. She loved her older brother, and felt that she would love his new wife too. When Marguerite came into the kitchen, Anna turned and kissed her new daughter-in-law. Emily pointed to the chair beside her and said, "You can sit here, beside me." The table was piled with bacon and eggs, toast and homemade strawberry jam, and an endless supply of coffee.

The war seemed very remote. In Ohio, there was general sympathy for Britain, but it seemed so far away. The Quaker community was deeply distressed that countries would resort to war. War caused nothing but suffering, destruction, and death. The depression in the US was over, and employment was on the increase again. The streams of unemployed workers had slowed and eventually stopped coming to town. The Quakers closed their soup kitchen that had served the destitute for ten years. The drought had long broken, and Ohio's fertile fields were in bloom. Life resumed its old patterns but it would never be quite the same, for the scars of the depression were deep.

Henry and Marguerite moved into a small house on the edge of Grandfather Hill's farm. It was a lovely little white house with flowers around the front steps. It had two bedrooms and a bath upstairs; a large kitchen and living room downstairs. There was a small garden in the back. Henry went back to the local college to finish his degree. He worked part-time for his grandfather in lieu of rent. Marguerite settled into the routine of the community, and was soon asked to help teach a morning class of pre-schoolers. It was hard for her, as English was not her first language, but she learned quickly. She taught the children Icelandic songs and poetry, and she would tell the them delightful stories about Icelandic heroes. In the afternoons she helped Anna with canning and preserving.

One Sunday, in December, their world was shattered when the Japanese bombed Pearl Harbor. The United Sates was now at war. The next day Germany declared war on the US. Anna worried about George, and Marguerite worried about her parents.

The government implemented food and gas rationing, and travel was restricted. The Selective Service Act was passed and every man aged 18 through 45 had to register for the draft. The Quaker Meeting called a special meeting to discuss their traditional pacifist position. Younger members of the Meeting had not had to face such a choice before. It had been twenty years for others. Many felt that, as Quakers, they should have nothing to do with the draft, and refuse to register. To refuse to register with Selective Service meant a five-year jail term. Others felt they should register but refuse military service, and still others—a few— enlisted in the Army or Navy as noncombatants.

As a pacifist, Henry faced a real dilemma. He knew he would be drafted, but what to do? Marguerite was expecting a baby the next summer. Over several long evenings Henry, Uncle John and Grandfather Hill discussed their philosophical positions. John was a farmer with a family, so his chances of being drafted were slim. Grandfather Hill was too old. Although Henry was married and could claim an exemption, he didn't know how long that would last. He resigned his teaching job and went to work full time for his grandfather and uncle. The draft board accepted this, but made it clear that they might have to change his classification later.

One day in the spring, the FBI agent stopped at the farm to see Anna. She invited him in for coffee. They sat at the kitchen table and chatted. He wanted to know her situation and she told him, for she had nothing to hide. When he asked about George, she said she had not heard from him in over six months, and consequently had no idea what he was doing. She worried about him, of course. Emily came home from school, walked over to her mother and looked very hard at the FBI agent. He rose, thanked them and left. On his way out of town he stopped at Henry's house. Henry was working, so he chatted with Marguerite. Did she know about George? No, only that he was Henry's twin brother. She had never met him. Henry did get an occasional letter from him, but that was all. The FBI agent thanked her, and as he left he asked where he could find Henry. "He's over at Grandfather Hill's farm today, plowing," she said.

The agent thanked her again. At the farm he found Henry coming in from the fields. Henry told him that he hadn't heard from George in a long time, so had no idea what he was doing, but he hoped all was well. The agent seemed satisfied and drove back to the city. He knew that when he dealt with the Hills he would get honest answers. They were good people.

In August, Marguerite gave birth to a healthy boy, Lars Peter, named for his two grandfathers. The United States army landed troops in Iceland to protect the Atlantic shipping lanes. Mail and telephone connections were restored, which pleased Marguerite immensely.

The war started badly in the Pacific. The Japanese invaded Indonesia and overran Singapore and Hong Kong. The American Army was driven out of the Philippines. Then the Canadians and British conducted a disastrous raid on Dieppe, suffering heavy casualties.

The United States increased rationing, particularly sugar. There was little meat, except what farmers slaughtered for themselves. Chicken, fish, and vegetables were plentiful. Farm families used their own dairy products. In the spring, each family received a twenty-pound bag of sugar for canning. Nobody in the community went without. There was always plenty of food, but there was an extreme shortage of durable goods, spare parts, and clothing. Fats, oils, grease, and gasoline were also strictly rationed.

As the war progressed, the demands of the military increased. Even clothes were rationed. The local draft board reviewed all their exemptions and informed Henry that he would lose his farm exemption. He would either have to join the army or claim Conscientious Objector (CO) status. If he claimed 4E (CO) status he would be assigned to a nearby Civilian Public Service (CPS) camp. CO's received $2.50 per month and this was hardly enough to support his family.

The whole family gathered in grandfather Hill's kitchen. Marguerite was a little fearful, for she didn't know quite what would happen if Henry had to leave home. She was not the pacifist Henry was, and she was pregnant again. She worried how they would manage. Anna and John supported Henry.

Grandfather Hill bowed his head and said reverently, "Let us wait upon the Lord, for He will show us the Way." They sat in silent meditation. To Henry, the way was clear. He couldn't join the army, and a jail term was out of the question. Both families assured Marguerite that she was a much loved part of the family. She had nothing to worry about. They would take care of her and the children while Henry was in camp.

That night she telephoned her parents. She expressed her fears and worries. She suggested that Kajsa come to Ohio and live with her. Her parents thought that was a good idea. They were concerned about Kajsa's association with American troops stationed in Reykjavík, as they tended to be a hard-drinking, boisterous bunch. A trip to Ohio would broaden her horizons.

In due course Henry's classification was changed and he was ordered to report to the CPS camp at Coshocton, Ohio, 150 miles south. The war dragged on and life became increasingly difficult, particularly for older people. Grandfather Hill had to cull his herd, and kept only enough dairy stock to supply his own family and a few friends. John Hill could only find farm hands during harvest time, and then they were unreliable. This was the case with all the farms in the neighborhood. The harvest was a cooperative effort. Of those young men not drafted, many had relatively high-paying jobs in the city. Schools shared teachers and facilities. Fuel oil, for heating, was rationed; coal was scarce. If you had access to a woodlot, you were lucky, as kitchen stoves and fireplaces were pressed into service. Anna kept a flock of chickens and sold the eggs locally. Separation from Henry was hard on Marguerite, but she still taught the pre-schoolers in the morning while Anna took care of Lars. Other than growing and tending flowers, Marguerite had never done any vegetable gardening. With the Anna's help, she managed to grow a respectable garden.

Kajsa sailed on a supply ship to Halifax where a member of the Icelandic consulate met her, helped her clear customs, and saw her onto the train for Montreal. She had never seen a city like Montreal. It was terrifying, and everyone spoke French! She had trouble enough with English and couldn't understand or speak French. The ladies of the Traveler's Aid Society were most helpful, and put her on the train for Toronto and Buffalo. She explained to the US customs agents, as best she could, that she was going to Ohio to be with her sister. From Buffalo she took another train to Cleveland. Kajsa marveled at the distances, and so much space compared to the compact villages and countryside of Iceland.

Anna, Emily, Marguerite and baby Lars drove to Cleveland to meet the train. Anna had saved enough gas coupons for the trip. They were all waiting at the station platform as the train pulled in. On the drive home, Anna and Emily sat in front; Kajsa, Marguerite and the baby in the back.

Marguerite and Kajsa chattered happily in Icelandic all the way. Emily smiled. She had someone new to love and welcome into her growing family circle.

12

World War II

ON SEPTEMBER 1, 1939, Hitler spoke to the German *Reichstag* (Parliament). His mood was somber.

"In defense against Polish attacks, German troops moved into action against Poland at dawn today. This is not war, only an engagement to destroy terrorists."

The gray-green troops of the Fatherland poured out of the mists onto an unsuspecting populous. German newspapers proclaimed the right of the Fatherland to defend itself against the wicked Poles, who had attacked and destroyed a radio transmitter. The whole affair had been staged by the SS to look like an unprovoked attack. The Luftwaffe pounded the Polish airfields, destroying the antique planes of the Polish Air Force, which were lined up on the ground. Tanks moved swiftly ahead of the infantry, displaying a new type of warfare. In one corner of the country— Pomerania—there was a valiant but disastrous counterattack by the famed Polish Cavalry Division. It was a heroic charge, with pennants flying and sabres flashing, but they were no match for the might of the German panzers. Both men and horses were butchered.

In three weeks, the state of Poland ceased to exist as an obstacle to the German offensive. The SS-Gestapo rounded up the Jews and all other undesirables. The concentration camps were full. German industries, particularly Siemens and I.G. Faber, used these prisoners as forced labor. Troops of the Soviet Union moved into eastern Polish provinces, as provided by a recently signed nonaggression pact with Germany.

It was a busy time for the *Abwehr*, for they were already preparing for an invasion of the West. A number of weeks later, a submarine captain, reporting to *OKW*, saw George and the Admiral walking down the hall. He saluted, looked at George and said, "I'm glad to see you are back from your secret mission, and hope that the young lady is well."

Oh, thought George, *he must have seen Henry and Marguerite.* He answered, "Of course, all went according to plan, and the young lady is very well. Thank you for asking." The submarine captain saluted and went on down the hall.

Later, the Admiral asked George what he had been talking about. George explained that the submarine captain must have seen Henry, thought he was George, and Henry had concocted some story about a secret mission. The Admiral laughed and said, "Your brother is a brave man."

One morning, George was summoned to the Alexanderplatz Gestapo headquarters. He was put in a small windowless interrogation room with a desk and two chairs. On the wall was a picture of Hitler. His cousin Klaus, resplendent in his black and silver uniform, and another SS officer entered, saluted and sat down. George was left standing. The officer took a file out of his brief case.

"It's been reported," he said, "that you have been seen in the United States. Were you there?"

"No," George replied, "that was my twin brother and he lives in the United States. You can verify this with my Grandmother Herzberg, if you wish."

Klaus listened, and growled, "What he says is true, but I don't trust him. Carry on."

Klaus left, and the interrogation continued. George remained standing. The SS officer was finally satisfied and told George he was free to leave.

When George told the Admiral of the interview, he looked very grave. "We've got get you out of Germany as soon possible. I don't trust the SS. They are getting too nosy, and they don't trust you. They look on the *Abwehr* with suspicion. Besides, they're power hungry."

The invasion of Norway and Denmark was a prelude to the invasion of the western European countries. The lowlands were quickly overrun, and France capitulated in June with barely a fight. What was left of the British Expeditionary Force escaped by sea at Dunkirk. Hitler and the generals were jubilant. They were now certain that the British government would agree to peace terms and join them in their fight against the red menace, the Soviet Union. The British government rejected any peace offers from the *Fuhrer*. Hitler was furious. "How dare they defy me!" he barked. "I'll show them what Germans are made of. Don't they know they are defeated!"

Hitler ordered Heydrich to convene a conference of the Gestapo in Wannsee to discuss plans for a final solution to the Jewish problem. They were to be exterminated by any means possible. "The Jew is a blight on the German soul," he told them.

Gas chambers were installed in many of the concentration camps. This was a highly secret project, and the Gestapo was given carte-blanche to carry out these orders. Their first installment was the execution of the old, the feeble and infirm, who had been placed in poorhouse barracks for safekeeping. Then they turned their attention to the Jews in concentration camps. Most of them were to be rounded up and deported to various concentration death camps. The purification of Germany had begun.

Hitler called his high command together. He ranted and raved and demanded that England be smashed. Field Marshal Göring and his Luftwaffe were ordered to destroy the Royal Air Force (RAF). The bombing of Britain began, first the airfields and then the cities. The small RAF, with their Spitfires and Hurricanes, fought back, downing large numbers of German bombers.

When France surrendered, the Duke and Duchess of Windsor fled from France to Portugal. Hitler ordered the SS to meet with the Duke and convince him to move to Spain. They promised the Duke his throne back when Britain surrendered. The Duke had strong family ties with the Reich, and he spoke fluent German. He and the Duchess had visited Hitler before the war. Hitler was sure that the Duke would be willing to join the German cause, to unite against the Communists of the Soviet Union.

The British Government and Prime Minister Winston Churchill suspected something, for there seemed to be more than the usual activity in Lisbon. Churchill did not trust the SS and was uncertain about the Duke. He arranged to have the Duke and the Duchess spirited out of Portugal in the night, and taken to the Bahamas. The Duke was appointed Governor General for the islands, which he felt was an insult, but now both were safely out of the way for the duration of the war.

German armies invaded the Balkans, Greece and North Africa with little resistance. The forces of the *Axis* were on the march. All the while, the bombing of Britain continued. In the early spring Hitler called his High Command together. He told them he had changed his mind. They would not invade Great Britain, but they were to prepare for an invasion of Russia in June.

Hitler believed that, after the Jews, the Communists were the worst enemy of Europe. He had signed a nonaggression pact with the Soviet Union for his own purposes, to protect the eastern front during his invasion of Poland. He had not been very happy when the Red Army had expanded into the Baltic States and Romania. To him, this wasn't part of the agreement. He told the generals that when the Germans came, the Russian people would rise up in revolt against the Communists. The generals assured Hitler that it would be merely an eight-week campaign; the Soviet Union would capitulate by Christmas. As a result, the German armies were not equipped for winter fighting.

Three great armies attacked simultaneously, catching the Soviet Union off-guard. The Red Army was suffering from an earlier purge of its top generals and therefore had very few trained and experienced officers. Unfortunately, Hitler and his generals had no idea of the vast distances within Russia, the poor road conditions, and the terrible weather. Even the rail lines were of a different gauge. The General Staff and the commanding generals had been hoodwinked by Hitler into believing that they, and the *Wehrmacht* (German Armed Forces), were invincible.

Admiral Canaris and a few other officers were troubled. To him the overstuffed generals were heading down a very dangerous path. The Soviet Union was just too vast, with too many resources. The *Wehrmacht* couldn't begin to conquer and subdue the whole of the Soviet Union, and in the end they would be destroyed. All of the *Abwehr's* intelligence pointed to defeat, but the General Staff and the High Command wouldn't listen.

• • •

George woke up to the wailing of sirens. It was dark. He groped his way to the window. All was quiet and then, suddenly, there was one explosion, then another, followed by the whistling sound of other falling bombs. He dashed downstairs and out of the building. The antiaircraft guns fired into the night, and search lights probed the night sky above the city.

The first British bombing raid on Berlin had lasted all of fifteen minutes, and was rather ineffective. Among the few buildings hit, a boarding school had been destroyed. The following morning, newspaper headlines decried the raid:

> "Night crime of British against children.
> This bloody act cries for revenge."
> *Nachtausgabe* – the Night Edition of a newspaper

> "Murder of children at Bethal a revolting crime."
> *Deutsche Allgemeine Zeitung*
> (*German General Journal* – the leading German newspaper of the time)

The physical damage was slight, but the psychological damage was immense. Berlin, the capital of the Third Reich, had been bombed. Göring had boasted that the Luftwaffe would destroy the RAF, and no bombs would ever fall on Berlin. Now it had happened. The war was suddenly real. Over the following weeks, RAF night bombing became more and more accurate as more and more cities were targeted.

As the armies of the Reich rolled into Russia they met little resistance. Leningrad was surrounded, the towers of Moscow could be seen across the plain, and the famed Sixth Army rolled through the Ukraine. Their drive continued until it was halted at the Volga. Then the siege of Stalingrad began.

On the home front, the Gestapo-SS tightened its grip on power. The concentration camps were full. Executions had to be stepped up to make room for Russian prisoners. The gas chambers and the crematoriums in the great death camps—Auschwitz, Maidanek, and Treblinka—were in full operation. This was to be the final solution for all Jews, communists and other troublemakers.

The *Abwehr* was preoccupied with war on two fronts, one in Russia and the other in western Europe. The Vichy Government of France, under the former World War I Field Marshal, Henri-Philippe Pétain and the slippery Pierre Laval, was more authoritarian and anti-Semitic than the Nazis. Jews and left-wing Socialists were rounded up and sent to Dachau. Portugal was neutral, refusing to take sides. The capital, Lisbon, was the only free and open port in Europe. Every country maintained a full network of spies there.

The Admiral called George into his office. "We're going on a trip. I want to visit the *Abwehr* offices in France, Spain, and Portugal. I need an adjutant to handle all the routine business. So you are coming. I have several plans to discuss with you. The SS are asking too many questions, and it is time for you to leave the country. As you know, a group of us want to end this war while there is still time. Get your things together, we are traveling as civilians."

They made stops in Paris, Lyon, Vichy, Madrid, and finally, Lisbon. In Lyon they had to wait for their train to Vichy. The stationmaster suggested they walk over to the freight yard. He snarled that the damned Gestapo were deporting Jews. George and the Admiral stood in the shadow of the freight shed and watched the Gestapo cram hundreds of helpless people, mostly women and children, into freight cars and bolt the doors. The engine driver walked by and George asked him where the train was going. He answered simply, "Treblinka." The notorious death camp. George and the Admiral walked in silence back to the station to catch their train to Vichy.

The next day, the Admiral held conferences with the French Secret police. They were more militant and brutal than the Gestapo. This depressed the Admiral. On the long train trip over the Pyrenees, he sat bundled in a robe, deep in thought. He barely noticed Madrid, a routine stop on their way to Lisbon.

After they disembarked, George and the Admiral checked into an hotel and then registered with the German embassy before retiring for the night. The following day, the Admiral took George to a remote tavern on the beach for lunch. After they had eaten, they strolled along the sand. "George," said the Admiral, "you must get yourself to the American embassy as soon as you can. If anyone asks, you are on official business. Tell the Embassy who you are—just an American who wants to go home. Show them your American passport, and destroy all your German identification papers so no one can connect you with *Abwehr*. I have known for a long time that your sympathies were not completely with the Party, but you were too valuable to us. We were unable to break the code in your letters to Henry, although we tried. I am sure you kept him informed. You have been like the son I never had, and I will miss you. So now, it is goodbye. Good luck, and may God bless you, for I am leaving shortly to return by night train to Berlin. Please give my regards to your brother when you see him."

They shook hands. George felt a lump rise in his throat, for he was leaving a man he had come to like and respect. The Admiral turned and walked back along the beach. George watched him until he was out of sight. In a secluded spot, George built a small fire and burned all of his German identification papers, scattering the ashes in the sand.

George decided not to return to the tavern and instead went directly back to the hotel. Walking down the hotel corridor, he noticed that the door to his room was open. This alarmed George and he had determined to turn away and leave when maid came out with an armload of linens. She looked surprised to see him. "Oh sir, we were told that you had left and to clean the room. Two gentlemen were here earlier, looking for you."

George thanked her as he slipped her some money, then left the hotel via a back staircase. He had to pass a corner of the lobby to reach the back entrance through the kitchen. Two men in black coats were standing near the main entrance looking out onto the street. The Gestapo-SS didn't waste any time. He hurried through the kitchen and into the back alley. He had to reach the American Embassy as soon as possible, for his life was in real danger. He ducked in and out of the shadows and became just another man on the streets of Lisbon.

13

The Escape

EORGE WAS ON THE ALERT NOW, for his life was in real danger. He knew the Gestapo wanted to arrest him and question him. The Gestapo had never liked the Admiral, nor the *Abwehr*, and they had always felt that intelligence-gathering was their business. They were very suspicious of the Admiral's trip to Paris and points south and west.

The Admiral had returned to Berlin on the night train, alone. Where was George? For some time, the Gestapo had suspected George was a traitor and now the orders came from headquarters: Bring him back to Berlin.

George made his way cautiously along the streets and back alleys to the American Embassy. He didn't think he was being followed, but he wasn't sure. Remarkably, George reached the embassy unchallenged and went directly to the reception desk. He showed his American passport, and asked to see the ambassador. The duty officer was skeptical and showed George to small office. After a while an under-secretary appeared. George explained his situation to him, and was again told to wait. After a further hour, he was taken to the ambassador's office. Oh how he wanted to go home! The Ambassador rose and waved George to a chair.

"Please begin."

"I am George Hill. The FBI thinks I am a spy. The SS-Gestapo thinks I am a spy. Both groups would like to talk to me, and I have far more faith in the FBI than the Gestapo. My mother and twin brother live in Ohio. After my father's death in 1930, I stayed in Germany, but not by choice, with my Herzberg grandparents. I was brought up as a German and, if you ask if I am a Nazi, the answer is yes, because if I hadn't joined the Party I would now be in concentration camp or dead. You have no idea what it is like to live in an atmosphere of constant terror and fear." The ambassador's expression told him to continue.

"Because I am fluently trilingual, I attracted the attention of the *Abwehr*. Admiral Canaris acted as my patron. I hated the double-dealing and spying, but there was no way out. I kept up a lively correspondence with my twin brother, Henry, in Ohio. We devised a code which no one has succeeded in breaking, although both FBI and the *Abwehr* have tried. Between Henry and the Admiral, I was able to retain my sanity and not become a mindless Nazi robot.

"The SS-Gestapo is gaining more and more power over the German people, who are terrified as well as brainwashed. Germany is now ruled by a gang of ruthless thugs. Admiral Canaris foresaw that it was imperative for me to leave Germany and that is why I am here. He has returned to Berlin. The SS-Gestapo is after me now. They want to arrest me and take me back to Berlin where I will undoubtedly be questioned and imprisoned, quite likely tortured and possibly executed. The question is, how am I going to get to America?"

The Ambassador listened very carefully. He asked George all manner of questions, which George answered honestly. They talked seriously for three hours before the ambassador was satisfied. Finally he said, "George, you can't go back to your hotel. I'll send someone over to collect your things. Meanwhile, stay here."

"There is no need to check my room," George offered. "They have already cleaned it out."

Later that afternoon, a staff member came back and reported that all trace of George's or the Admiral's stay had disappeared from the hotel register. The SS-Gestapo were certainly thorough, and they were on the prowl, so George had to be very careful. Fortunately, he had his American passport and some money. The ambassador told him of a little pension around the corner, which the embassy used. George was to go there and stay out of sight until a staff member came for him in the morning. "You will be safe there," he added. "A ship is leaving for the US tomorrow night. It will be watched, I'm sure, but I think we can make it appear that you are one of the crew. Take care and I'll see you in the morning."

After breakfast, George stood in his room looking out the window, with the curtains not quite fully drawn. He saw a local police car pull up. Two policemen dressed green uniforms entered the pension. The landlady greeted them coolly. They said they were looking for an escaped criminal wanted by the SS. The landlady threw up her hands, screaming at the police that she didn't keep that kind of pension. "Who in the name of God do you think you are!" she shouted. "You're nothing but a pair of dumb cops, you'd better clear off!"

The police, looking a little embarrassed, begged her humble pardon and left with their caps in their hands. As the police car drove away, a black, unmarked car followed. Then an embassy staff member, who had been watching from a doorway, crossed the street and slipped into the building.

Soon there was a knock at the door. After George had identified the staff member through a tiny lens in the door, he allowed him to enter. "I see we've already had visitors," he said quietly. "Here are your clothes, a new set of identification papers, and a French passport. The dock area is about a half mile down the road. If anyone stops you, answer only in French. Remember, you are a French sailor going to your ship. We'll keep an eye on you. Good luck."

George changed his clothes, packed his knapsack, and went out the back door into the alley. He looked like a common sailor with a two-day stubble. In and out of the shadows in the alley he walked, pausing at the corners to check the street ahead. He could see the *Excambion* tied up at the pier. As he neared the dock area, George noticed a man on the other side of the street. He wore neat civilian clothes and a grey trench coat. George stepped into a doorway and lit a cigarette. Something was wrong. As the man went into the booking office, a black car swooped down the street. Two men jumped out, rushed in, hauled the man out and threw him into the back seat. After they slammed the door and roared off, George moved quietly from one doorway to the next. He noticed another man in a black coat leaning against some barrels and watching the booking office. George walked up to him and asked, "Eh, avez vous une cigarette?"

The man looked bewildered and fumbled in his pockets, then slumped into George's arms. He never knew what hit him—a well-aimed karate chop. George dragged him behind a pile of lumber and frisked him. He took his pistol and money, tore up his identification papers and threw the pieces in the water. Then he stepped out from behind the lumber pile, looked around and moved toward the ship. He spotted another "black coat" standing near the back of the booking office and looking out to sea. Silently, George walked up behind him and pushed him into the water. The booking office was a trap. He turned and ran down the dock, then up the gangplank. Once on the deck, he turned just in time to see four more black coats rush into the booking office.

George moved from one companion way to the next until he arrived on the bridge. He asked the first mate, who was looking out the window, to call the captain. The mate just laughed and shrugged his shoulders. George moved in swiftly and planted his pistol in the mate's back. "You will call the captain or you will be a cripple for life. I will blow out your spine." The mate turned a sickly white and called the captain.

The captain was a tall, thin man with intense grey eyes and a weather-beaten face. He understood the situation immediately. "We were expecting you, but you didn't have to be quite so rough."

"When the Gestapo are after you, you have to be rough. They're swarming all over the dock, and if you let them or the local police on this ship, they will tell you they're searching for a fugitive from justice."

The captain nodded and showed George where he could hide until they sailed. George apologized to the mate, who nodded weakly.

The captain and the first mate stationed themselves at the top of the gangplank. A captain with the Lisbon police, wearing a starched green uniform and shiny black boots, led a squad of his men up the gangplank and demanded to search the ship. The ship's captain suggested to the police captain that the two of them retire to the wardroom for some refreshment and discuss this whole matter, "like gentlemen" while the others remained on deck.

The police captain accepted the invitation and, after some excellent wine, he complained about "those damned Germans" and how he wished they would go home; for he and his men, they represented nothing but trouble. They had found one agent in the water and another unconscious and the Gestapo were demanding an explanation, although he knew that his friend, the ship's captain, would never harbor a fugitive. Glasses were refilled and more toasts were made, and they departed with smiles and handshakes all around. A case of wine was thoughtfully provided to the police squad who subsequently reported they had "seen and heard nothing."

That afternoon, the passengers came aboard and the ship sailed with the tide. They gave George a small cabin in steerage, and told him to stay out of sight. The danger wasn't over, for they still had to cross the Atlantic.

George was walking on deck one morning, when a German submarine surfaced off the port bow. He quickly went to his cabin and locked the door. The submarine boarding party hailed the ship and asked permission to come aboard. Permission granted, the sub's first officer went into the wardroom with the ship's captain. The officer wished to inspect the passenger and crew manifests. He went over the lists with great care, then stood up, saluted, and said they could proceed. The ship's captain asked who they were looking for. The reply was, "A member of the *Abwehr* who is trying to defect, and we heard he was on board a ship." Then the sub's first officer stood up, clicked his heals, saluted again and left the ship. George, who had been lying on his bunk with his pistol at the ready, heard the engines start up. He sighed with relief.

A few minutes later there was a knock on his door and the captain came in. "They're gone, but they are after you."

"I know."

"Oh, by the way, it came over the wireless just now, that the Gestapo has arrested Admiral Canaris and several other high ranking German staff Generals, and charged them with treason."

"Oh no," George said. "He is such a good man, and a good loyal officer. They'll kill him for certain."

As the captain turned to leave he said, "Two more days and we'll be in New York. Lie low till then. Incidentally, your name does not appear on any manifest."

◆ ◆ ◆

When George woke up, his first thought was how he was going to manage in New York. A steward brought him a suitcase of clean clothes and a garment bag with an overcoat and hat. "The captain is expecting you for breakfast," he said. "It will be served in the wardroom in an hour."

George showered and shaved off his ten days of stubble. Then he put on his new suit and went up to the wardroom. The captain was already at the table and waved him to a seat. It was a wonderful breakfast of fruit, bacon, eggs, toast and coffee.

"George, I would advise you to use your own passport. Immigration will collect them just before docking. Don't worry about your suitcase. I'll ship it to you later. You just get home to Ohio as fast as you can. The FBI will catch up with you soon enough, and better in Ohio than New York."

"Thank you for everything," George said, with gratitude and relief in his voice.

"Don't worry." The captain smiled. "I was well paid for it, and it was a pleasure. I am no fan of the Gestapo."

They stood and shook hands.

George packed his suitcase and threw some of his old clothes in the trash. Dressed in his new overcoat and hat, he turned in his passport to the immigration officer. The officer glanced at it and put in it the sack at his side. They were docking in New York harbor!

Down the gangplank George strode, through customs and out to the taxi rank. It was a short trip to Penn Station. *The Jeffersonian*, the Pennsylvania Express to St. Louis, left within an hour. How glad he was to be on his way home!

When George alighted in Barnesville he asked the way to his mother's house, and was directed to the farm. He entered the kitchen quietly and saw his mother working at the sink. Emily saw him and tugged at her mother's skirt. Anna turned just as George said, "Mother!"

"What are you doing here, Hen—George!" She flew into his arms. After a long embrace and tears on both sides, Anna wiped her eyes. "Oh George, my son! I never expected to see you again. Sit down and I'll call Henry."

George sat down at the kitchen table while Anna went to the phone. Emily watched him carefully. She walked around the table, looked up at him and said solemnly, "You look just like my brother Henry. Do you know him?"

"Oh yes, he is my brother too."

Emily didn't know how this could be, but she would ask her mother. Anna called Henry and asked him to come over as she had a surprise for him. Henry rode over to the farm on a tractor, wondering what his mother wanted. When he entered the kitchen, he saw George. The two embraced without words, just too happy to see each other again. Emily stood close to her mother, studying the two men. Intuitively she could tell them apart. She walked over to them and Henry stooped to hug her. She reached out to George and hugged him too. Anna's joy was complete—both her boys were home again.

• • •

It was a joyous dinner at Hill's farm that night. Grandfather Hill gave thanks: "Heavenly Father we thank thee for the safe return of our George and for the blessings thee has bestowed upon us."

George was delighted to meet his new sister-in-law and little Lars. It was so wonderful to be part of a loving family again. He didn't realize how much he had missed it, but here he was surrounded by love.

• • •

A sack of passports arrived at the State Department and were duly sorted. George Hill's passport was forwarded to the FBI. The Cleveland office was alerted. The agent in charge of the Hill file called Anna and told her that he would come by the next day. When he arrived, Anna met him at the kitchen door and said that George was in the living room. The agent opened the door and saw the twins sitting on the chesterfield. He looked from one to the other, frowned, studied them again, and smiled.

"You're George," he said pointing to one of them.

"How did you know?"

"Henry has a wedding ring on and you don't, and I've met Henry's wife. That was the only way I could tell you two apart."

The twins smiled. Henry excused himself and went back to work. The agent and George spent all morning in the living room with the door shut. At noon Anna knocked on the door to say that lunch was ready. After lunch the conversation continued well into the afternoon.

George was not the pacifist that Henry was. He was perfectly willing to work for the FBI and the US government, but he would not join the army. Over the next several weeks he attended many consultations in Cleveland, Washington, and on the farm. He willingly shared with the FBI his knowledge of Germany and the German intelligence service. He hated the Gestapo for what they had done to the Admiral. In this way he was able to redeem his soul.

14

George and Ann

THE WAR CONTINUED. The Allies conducted round-the-clock bombing of Germany. The British Eighth Army drove Rommel out of North Africa. The Red Army advanced steadily toward Berlin. The famed German Sixth Army, trapped on the Volga, defied Hitler's direct orders and surrendered at Stalingrad. Field Marshal Paulus and his generals went to prison in Siberia. An assassination attempt on Hitler failed. Admiral Canaris and the other conspirators were arrested, tortured, and hanged by the Gestapo.

The flowers in the White House rose garden were in full bloom. George had been called to a conference with the President in the Oval Office. In attendance were the Secretary of State, the Chief of the General Staff, and the head of the Office of Strategic Services (OSS). The invasion of Europe was the agenda.

The Allies wanted to arrest all members of the Gestapo and Nazi Party and bring them to trial. They were worried that some of the high-ranking members would escape justice. Interrogators were required, especially those who had an intimate knowledge of Germany and were fluent in the language. George was to go back to Britain and organize a corps of interrogators. They offered him an officer's rank, but he refused. He preferred to remain a civilian.

George boarded a cold transport plane in New York, sharing space with a cargo of spare parts. When the plane put down in Reykjavík for refueling, George went for a walk out on the tarmac. He was stretching his legs and admiring the sunset when he heard someone call "Henry!" He turned to see a man approaching. Lars Pederson, the harbormaster—who often took a shortcut via the airfield en route from home to his office at the harbor—had seen George and mistook him for Henry.

George explained that he was Henry's twin brother, and on his way to Britain. Lars insisted that he come home for dinner and tell them the news of Marguerite and the baby. George checked with the pilot; they wouldn't be taking off until dawn.

The three sat around the Pederson table visiting and eating supper. Katherine was eager to know of her new grandson. The news that Marguerite was expecting another baby caused much excitement. It was a wonderful evening. George thanked them warmly and promised to return to Iceland whenever he could.

Early the next afternoon, the American plane landed in fog and drizzle on a RAF airbase outside London. George was met and immediately driven to a meeting with the General Staff. When he walked in, he recognized the staff officer he had met before the war.

"Oh I say, you do get around, don't you," the officer remarked. "You know, I could swear I saw you in Portsmouth a couple of days after you were last here."

"You saw my twin brother. He was on his way home." George didn't volunteer information about his previous mission.

Later that same afternoon, he met with the intelligence personnel in charge of interrogating prisoners, and that evening he made inquiries about Ann Catchpool. Her family had left London before the Blitz, but no one was sure were Ann lived or where she worked. Someone thought that she was serving in a radar unit, somewhere on the southeast coast.

• • •

Ann Catchpool was a striking young woman. She often wondered what had become of her handsome American. She dreamed of meeting him again. Remembering the evening at the theater made her feel warm all over. The Catchpool family had moved out to the suburbs, and Ann had taken a job at one of the coastal radar stations. She was lonely, and had no close friends. The girls she knew were either married or engaged to servicemen. She thought about George and how the Americans had quite a contingent of troops and airmen in Britain.

On the day after George arrived, she reported to duty as usual. Everything was fairly routine, now that the German bombings had slacked off. An orderly knocked on her office door with a message. A chap named George Hill had called, and had left his phone number. Was this her handsome American? Ann felt a flutter inside. She dialed London and asked for George Hill. The duty officer told her that he was in conference, and would probably be engaged all day. She left her phone number and her location. She felt a little disheartened when she hung up the phone. Perhaps this wasn't her American after all.

• • •

A few days later there was a knock on her office door. There stood George, holding a bouquet of flowers. Suddenly Ann felt shy, and she blushed because her uniform was rumpled and her makeup needed attention. It *was* her handsome American, and what would he think of her? George smiled. He was glad he had found her; he had often thought of her since that delightful evening at the theater, back in 1939.

Soon they were chatting easily. At tea break, they walked across the compound to the canteen, and when their hands touched, they exchanged a look that held them for a wonderful moment. George told her he had to go back to London for a conference, but he would return the next day, and could they have dinner together? Ann's spirits soared as she listened to this exciting young man.

The next evening, Ann, looking radiant in her best dress, met George at the station. Her heart quickened just to see him again. They had dinner in the small dining room of the Crown and Stag. The innkeeper saw the glances that passed between them, and provided a secluded table. They enjoyed roast beef and Yorkshire pudding at their leisure, and afterwards walked along the coastal road. Throughout that long June evening they basked in a glow neither of them could hide.

On the weekend, Ann took George to visit her parents. Frank and Gwen Catchpool welcomed George into their home, a small semidetached house in the suburbs, with a little vegetable garden in the side yard. The

Catchpool's wanted to know of George's family in Ohio. He showed them family pictures of Henry and his mother. Frank had been in France during the Great War doing reconstruction work, and Gwen had served as a nurse in a French maternity hospital.

Later, George told Ann that once the invasion took place, he would be very busy, and might have to go over to the continent. He couldn't tell her precisely what he did, but simply said he was "with intelligence."

• • •

June 6, the day of the great armada. American, British and Canadian troops landed on the beaches of Normandy. Within days, they had moved inland, securing their positions. The Germans put up fierce resistance, but were out-gunned and outmaneuvered. George's corps of interrogators fanned out over France. George went to Paris to supervise. While sitting at a sidewalk cafe enjoying a coffee, he saw a man he knew. "Hans!"

The man turned, recognized George, and grinned. It was Hans Schmitt, chief of the Gestapo in northern France. George knew he was taking a chance, because this man was considered the most dangerous and vicious of the Gestapo chiefs.

"So here you are," Hans said smiling. "We wondered where you were. We lost track of you in Lisbon. Too bad the Waffen-SS has retreated. What have you been doing?"

George replied, evading the question. "What happened to the SS? You're not in uniform?"

"The Americans are so stupid, they couldn't catch any of us if they fell over us."

George smiled to himself. "How about a drink, Hans? I know a nice out-of-the-way bistro."

"Oh, all right, just one, before I go back to headquarters. I'm leaving for Germany tonight."

George led the way to a little bistro on a side street. They sat at one of the sidewalk tables under a brightly-colored umbrella. George went in, ordered drinks and gave a signal to the bartender.

Like most SS, Hans was arrogant and overbearing, boasting of his prowess in eluding arrest. Unnoticed, three military policemen slipped up behind him and arrested him. Hans was furious and demanded his rights, then reached over his head for a knife. But the sergeant grabbed his arm and bent it behind his back.

"Hans, if you make one false move, you'll wish you were dead." George was aiming his pistol directly at him.

"Arrest him too!" Hans screamed, pointing at George.

".You never respected anyone else's rights. Why should we respect yours?"

Hans yelled and swore at the police as they handcuffed and frisked him, finding quite a collection in his pockets—money, a false passport, forged identification papers, a pistol, two sheath knives, and a bunch of keys. George gave the pistol and knives to the bartender. The police took the rest.

"Why don't you arrest him? He is a Nazi spy!" Hans kept screaming.

"Sorry Hans, you're on the wrong side," George said calmly. Then to the MP in charge, "Thanks, sergeant, for being so prompt. We've wanted him for a long time."

"You traitor! We always knew you were a traitor—you and that sniveling Canaris." Hans continued his ranting and raving as the MP's dragged him off to jail.

George pocketed his pistol and heaved a sigh of relief. Then he paid for the drinks, thanked the bartender and left. He flew back to London, and that night slept in his own bed. He hated this double dealing and wished that he and Ann were in Ohio. The next day he called Ann and asked her to come up to London for the weekend.

It was like a holiday! They walked through Kew Gardens, dined out, and enjoyed the theater. On Sunday, Ann took George to the Quaker Meeting House at Jordans. "William Penn is buried in the cemetery," she said, leading him to the spot.

George stared at the grave without speaking. Finally he said, "You know, William Penn asked George Fox how long he should wear his sword. And the reply was, 'As long thou canst.' Tomorrow I am going to turn in my sidearms, as I have no need for them anymore. There is enough evil in the world now, and I don't have to add to it."

Ann took his hand and held it tightly. She had never heard him talk like this before. George went on. "I'm going to resign from the intelligence service and try to bring some peace and light to people who have lived so long in darkness. Revenge is rampant and it only breeds hatred and more violence. Ann, dear, will you help me?" He took Ann in his arms and kissed her. Her response was pure passion.

When they had tea at the Catchpool home, Ann told her parents of their plans. They reported to work on Monday and each submitted a letter of resignation. The Intelligence Service refused to accept George's letter. They didn't mind if he gave up his sidearms, but his linguistic talents made him far too valuable. After several hours of heavy discussion they agreed that he would remain in Britain to head the language school. This was a compromise George could accept.

That evening he talked it all over with Ann. She saw the wisdom in the compromise and agreed. Then they made plans for their wedding, which would be in two weeks. George wrote long letters to his mother and Henry telling them all the news. Anna wrote a very warm, welcoming reply to Ann. She was delighted to have another daughter-in-law. The Catchpool's arranged to have the wedding in their local Meeting. It was a very simple ceremony, although a few friends and neighbors also attended and helped to make it a memorable celebration.

◆ ◆ ◆

The Allied armies pushed the demoralized Germans back over the Rhine. The Red Army occupied Berlin. The major German cities were in ruins. Hitler and some of his inner circle of Nazi generals committed suicide; others were captured. In the spring, the German General Staff accepted an unconditional surrender. The thousand-year dream of the National Socialists had come crashing down. The German people were bewildered and confused, as if they were awakening from a ten-year nightmare.

Part of the Herzberg estate—their uncle's farm—and a nearby town were now located within the Russian zone. Fortunately, the family house and adjacent fields were within the British zone of occupation. A new road had to be built from a neighboring town to the Herzberg farmhouse across the British-held zone and George received permission from the British Occupation Command to check on his grandmother and aunts, for he had not heard from them in quite some time.

The Command lent him a Jeep to drive to the farm. As George drove into the yard he could see the house and grounds were deserted. Inside, the kitchen was dark and gloomy. There was no fire in the stove and the room smelled of decay. Even the cuckoo clock had stopped. George didn't notice his grandmother huddled in her chair, rocking slowly back and forth. She had lost so much weight her clothes hung on her. Her face and hands were dirty and grey. The pale aunts were nowhere to be found.

Grandmother looked up and saw him. "Oh George, where have you been?" she whined. "The Russians were here and have stolen everything. They took my girls with them, but I was too old to stop them. What could I have done?"

George shook his head sadly, for there was nothing to say. He found an old coat to wrap around her. Then he drove her to the rehabilitation center, where she would be cared for, and returned himself to Army Headquarters. He wrote to his mother about conditions at the farm, adding that "Grandmother adamantly refuses your help. It is so hard to help a person who refuses to be helped! At this time, I have no idea where your two sisters might be or what has befallen them."

George returned to Britain with a heavy heart. That evening, after supper, he told Ann the story of his family. Of his father and mother and his twin brother. Of his work with the *Abwehr*. Of his faith in the Admiral, his hatred of the Nazis. He hid nothing. He loved Ann so much, and wanted her to know everything. Ann took him in her arms and held him as he talked. He felt a great weight lifting from his shoulders. He didn't have to pretend anymore. He could be George Hill. That night they fell asleep holding each other very close.

George and Ann worked at the language school until the troops came home again—all over the world.

15

The Pale Aunts

THE WAR WAS OVER. For many, the nightmare was a terrible memory; for others, the nightmare was just beginning. Dreams had been dashed and all but forgotten. It had been a struggle of monumental proportions, and now Germany lay in ruins. The world recoiled at the conditions discovered in the concentration camps: piles of bones, desiccated bodies, and a few pitiful, starving survivors. The US and the Soviet Union emerged as the world's superpowers.

The pale aunts returned to the deserted farm with nothing. They had managed to survive their long ordeal in the Russian zone. They had been kidnapped, raped, humiliated, spat upon, and then discarded by the conquering Russians. They walked home, hiding in the woods or sleeping in deserted barns during the day, and walking at night. They were scared, and sometimes they didn't know where they were. Smashed or disfigured road signs added to their confusion. Many towns were in ruins, and roaming gangs of former soldiers prayed on innocent civilians—all this added to their grief. The aunts begged or stole food just to stay alive. It was a frightening experience and every incident delayed their return. They had no news of their brother, whom they presumed was still a prisoner of the Russians. Klaus, their nephew, had disappeared.

When they reached the farm, it was dark and deserted. The kitchen was cold and dreary, but on the table they found a letter from George saying that he had placed their mother in the rehabilitation center, and that she was suffering from dementia. The aunts walked into town to see her, but she barely recognized them. She just raved about being rescued. They left her at the center, where she would have better care, and went down the street to the relief agency. After describing their situation, the agency gave them some vegetable seeds, a bag of food and two bags of coal.

With these treasures the aunts walked back to the farm. They lit the stove, and rejoiced as the warmth filled the room. They were tired and dirty; what clothes they had, were filthy and torn. They found a couple of dresses in an upstairs closet, which had been overlooked by the looters, and some turnips in the cold cellar. After a wash and a change of clothes they cooked a meager supper. They dragged and pushed the big double bed into the kitchen, and started the cuckoo clock. It was the only warm room in the house. The rest of the house looked like a disaster.

The next day, after planting the garden, they walked into town for a few more bags of coal. They didn't expect any letters, but they were hoping to hear from their brother. There was another letter from George! He had sent them pictures of his wedding to Ann, and £100 sterling. This was a godsend. Now the aunts could buy food. Back at home they wrote him a long letter describing their adventures and what they had found at home. They closed by thanking him for helping them and their mother.

One day they were sitting at lunch, when a tall, gaunt man, wearing a ragged old army uniform, walked into the yard. He was carrying a small package and a letter for the aunts. They invited him to share their lunch. He thanked them, and after lunch he began to talk.

"I met your brother in basic Army training. He talked about his farm and how worried he was that he wasn't there. He worried about you and your mother, and the farm. We were assigned to the same artillery observation unit on the Eastern Front. This didn't involve much fighting. Our army retreated slowly, inflicting as much damage as it could. The Russian bombardment was continuous, and we were no match for them. They had fresh supplies and we did not. Our rations and ammunition supplies were cut. We had food for one meal a day and soon that was cut too. One night as we lay in our trench, your brother made me promise that if he died before the war was over I would take his ashes and this letter back to your mother.

"That night, the Russian bombardment was devastating. In the early dawn we retreated again, tried, hungry, dirty, and beaten. Our artillery unit was smashed. Many of the men and officers tore the insignia off their uniforms, and simply walked away. They could not stand the constant bombardment. Your brother and I slipped away in the night, back towards Berlin. Unfortunately, we ran into a Russian patrol and were thrown into jail.

"We had to work repairing roads, twelve hours a day, in all kinds of weather. We had very few tools, and at times we had to work with our hands. Your brother caught a severe cold, which turned into pneumonia. The Russians didn't care. Your brother struggled to keep up with the rest of us, but it was too much for him and he collapsed and coughed himself to death. I was able to slip his letter to you inside my shirt.

"That night I made a fire and cremated his body. What ashes there were, I stuffed into a pair of his old socks. The war was over, for us anyway. The surrender had been signed, and the Russians simply opened the gates of the prison and told us to go home. I had nothing, no food, just worn out shoes and tattered, dirty clothes. I walked all the way here, and I still have a long way to go."

He sighed and drank the last of his coffee. They buried the ashes of their brother at the bottom of the garden, and marked the grave with a small stone. The aunts urged the traveler to stay the night. He thanked them, but said he had to be on his way.

The aunts were very sad when he left, for now they had only each other. What were they to do? They didn't have the knowledge, capability or money to run the farm. Most of the farmland had gone fallow, fields were overgrown, fences broken, barns in disrepair, and the house was in dire need of repairs, cleaning and painting. Only their neat little garden showed any recent signs of care. They walked into town to visit their mother. The old lady, lost in her dementia, didn't even know they were there. And the aunts didn't know where to turn. In desperation, they wired George in Great Britain, asking his advice.

George and Ann were packing to leave for Ohio. Their work in Britain finished, they were going home by way of Iceland. When the desperate telegram from the aunts arrived, they postponed their trip for two weeks and received clearance from the British Occupation Command to visit Germany. A transport plane flew them to the British headquarters in northern Germany, and a staff car was provided to travel to the farm.

The aunts were overjoyed to see George and Ann. George looked around the farm, then drove to town to talk with the local land commissioner. That night, over supper, they discussed the possibility of selling the farm. Grandmother Herzberg, whose dementia was well advanced, still talked of being rescued by the valiant Imperial German Army and her dear Heinrich. She was totally unaware of anybody else or her present surroundings.

The Land Commission was eager to have farms for the many displaced persons that were swarming back into the country. They offered the aunts the current rate in cash. The Herzberg estate had been in the family for generations, but now there was no one to tend to it. Better it was sold and farmed than left idle. The next question was where the aunts would go. George wired his mother. The telegram came back that her sisters would be welcome to come to Ohio.

Thus, the farm was sold. The next day Grandmother Herzberg had a stroke and fell into a deep comma; within a week she was dead. They buried her next to their brother, at the bottom of the garden. After the funeral, George introduced the aunts to the local British commander. With George's help, passports, visas, tickets and travel papers were obtained. The red tape seemed endless. After much discussion and further questioning, passage was arranged for them on a refugee boat. George and Ann went back to Great Britain.

A month went by, and the aunts had heard nothing. One day a British Army truck came by the farm, picked up the aunts and their pitiful belongings, and took them to Wilhelmshaven. The aunts left the family farm with sadness, for this was the only home they had ever known. Each took a small suitcase. Each had a money belt hidden under her dress. They had no hats, no gloves, only light summer overcoats. They were leaving their childhood lives behind and heading to an unknown future, in a strange land.

A dirty freighter named *Vulture* lay tied up at the dock. The aunts were lucky that they had special clearance from the British Occupation Army. MPs controlled the gangplank, allowing only those with permits to board. The dock was crowded with refugees, all pressing to get on the boat. Pickpockets were having a field day. One brash youth snatched the suitcase from one aunt and ran away. She started after him, but her sister grabbed her arm.

"Stop, let it go, or else we'll miss the boat."

"But mother's gold watch is in the suitcase."

"Too bad."

The aunts hurried up the gangplank. A ship's officer examined their papers and assigned them two bunks in a small cabin, which they shared with two others. The ship was overcrowded. People slept anywhere: on the deck, in the hold, or in one of the lifeboats.

The *Vulture* weighed anchor and wallowed out to sea. If the food was terrible, the voyage was worse. The aunts alternated between their bunks and the deck. They were sick and miserable, they didn't know where they were going and, at that point, they didn't care!

After two weeks at sea the *Vulture* docked in Philadelphia. Everyone was ordered on deck, and told to assemble under the letter of their last name once the ship docked and they were allowed to disembark. These large letters hung from the ceiling of a quayside warehouse. The aunts clutched their few belongings and went down the gangplank. A dock official pointed to their letter. They were scared, because it was all so strange and foreign, and very few people spoke German.

The immigration officials began the slow work of processing the refugees. The aunts huddled together, awaiting their turn. The immigration officer looked at their papers and asked, "Do you have any relatives in the US?"

"Ja, our sister lives in Ohio," answered the aunt who knew a little English.

"What is her name, and where does she live?"

"Her name is Anna Hill and lives in Barnesville, Ohio."

"Does she know you are here?"

"No, but George knew we were coming."

"Who's George?"

"He is Anna's son."

"Where is he?"

"We think he still in UK."

The immigration officer thought for awhile, and then asked,

"Are you ladies perhaps Quakers?"

"No. Anna is."

The immigration officer smiled, turned to speak to another officer, and then said, "Would you ladies please wait over there."

It was a small room, with comfortable chairs and a table. A young stewardess served them coffee and pastry.

They sat there wondering what they were going to do, when a small lady bustled in and introduced herself to the aunts as Mary Jones. She shepherded them through customs and immigration, then led them out of the dockyards and up the street to the Arch Street Friends Center. They were shown to a nice clean bedroom with a bath. Mary Jones said she had wired Anna, and expected an answer soon. After they bathed they were to come down one floor to the dining room for lunch. The aunts sat on the bed, held each other and cried. Everything seemed so strange and different.

They each had a lovely hot bath and dressed in semi-clean dresses. Mary Jones joined them for luncheon. "This afternoon we will go shopping, for I am sure that you have very little in the way of clothes. Now is there anything you need in particular?"

One aunt blushed profusely and rattled off something in German to her sister.

"We need to wash our underclothes," said the one who spoke English.

"Of course, how foolish of me not to think of that," Mary said. "Just put them all in a pillow slip and give it to the maid on the floor. She will have them back by breakfast time tomorrow."

The aunts went to the bank, where the exchange rate added to their disappointment, but not to their meager supply of money: 9,000 Reichsmark was now worth only $900. They shopped at Gimbel's, buying new dresses, hose, shoes, new overcoats and new handbags. Mary suggested the hairdresser, which the aunts declined. But they did purchase a new suitcase to carry everything. When they attempted to pay, Mary said it was all paid for from a refugee fund.

The next morning at breakfast, Mary produced two tickets on the Pennsylvania railroad for Ohio. Anna had wired the money. A trolley car trip uptown took them to Penn Station. They said goodbye to Mary, thanked her for her kindness and boarded the train. Then they found a seat in the coach and hugged each other for joy. They couldn't quite believe what was happening. The train rolled through the Pennsylvania countryside, with stops in Harrisburg and Pittsburgh. Nine hours later the train reached Barnesville, Ohio. Standing on the platform were Anna, Emily, and Henry. What a joyous reunion it was that night. Only George and Ann were missing.

Emily slipped up beside Marguerite and took her hand. She watched these new aunts with interest. They were thin and drawn with haunted eyes. Her mother and brother were speaking a strange language. She pulled at Marguerite's sleeve and asked in a hushed voice, "Why are they scared?"

"They have had a very hard time," Marguerite replied, "and a long and difficult trip. They have never been away from their home before."

Emily watched and wondered. It had been a strange time. First Henry came home with his new wife, Marguerite; then Kajsa arrived, then George; now the two pale aunts with scared and haunted eyes. George and his new wife, Ann, were coming soon. Life was just one surprise after another.

16

The Further Adventures
of George and Ann

EORGE AND ANN RETURNED FROM GERMANY, well satisfied with what they had accomplished. The pale aunts were on their way to Ohio. Now they could finish their own packing and ship their trunks.

During a break from their packing, they were resting in the garden when an American officer knocked on the gate. He was very formal as he handed George an envelope. The letter contained orders for George to report to Nuremberg. This was a blow. The war trials were starting. A number of high-ranking Nazis were on trial for war crimes and misdemeanors against humanity. George was to be a translator and interpreter at the trials. He turned to Ann and shook his head.

"It might be for the best if you went ahead to Ohio. My family are looking forward to us coming and will be disappointed if neither of us arrives as we planned. I'll join you just as soon as the trials are finished."

Ann looked at her husband. "George, my beloved, where you go, I will go. I could not bear to be parted from you. This assignment will be extremely difficult, for you will see people on trial you knew in your former life, and old memories will come alive. I am afraid some very hateful and hurtful things will be said, or will happen. You will need all the support I can give you. So we will go together. Remember, I love you!"

George took Ann in his arms and held her very close. How could he be so lucky to have such a wonderful wife?

George reported to army headquarters the next morning. The colonel behind the desk handed him his ticket and said he was to leave in two days. George looked at the ticket and said, "There is only one ticket here. My wife is accompanying me, so she'll need a ticket too."

The colonel blinked. "We never send couples on assignment."

"Then, I will not go," George replied.

"But you are under orders."

George stood his ground and informed the colonel that he was a civilian. He would go to Nuremberg only if his wife went with him. Otherwise he was going home to Ohio. The colonel blustered and fumed. This was most unusual. They needed George badly, for the trials were not going well.

"Come back tomorrow, and I'll have an answer for you." Then he added, "And bring your wife with you."

George went home and told Ann what had happened.

The next morning they were ushered into a larger office. Seated behind the table was the colonel, looking glum, and a grey-haired staff general. They rose as George and Ann entered; Ann, perfectly dressed and looking radiant. The grey-haired general directed most of his questions to her. The colonel sat silent throughout the proceedings.

At the end of the interview the officers rose. The staff general shook hands with George and Ann, and commended Ann on her knowledge and poise. He was more than happy to have them both onside. The colonel glowered. It was obvious that he had been overruled. As they left the room, his tone was icy when he said their tickets and papers would be ready in the morning.

George wired Anna to explain their delay and asking her to please pick up their trunks at the station.

The skies were grey when they left London, but had cleared somewhat by the time they arrived in Nuremberg. They reported to the Judge Advocate General's office. The duty officer was very helpful with identity cards, passes, and food ration cards. When all the paperwork was finished, he took a ring of keys out of a drawer, beckoning George and Ann to follow. They walked down the main street, then turned up a side street.

The duty officer unlocked a bright yellow door and ushered them in. It was a small house of two floors, furnished very nicely. Downstairs, a living room and kitchen-dining area flanked the hall; upstairs, a bedroom on one side and a small dressing room and bathroom on the other. The living room looked out onto a little flower garden.

"I hope this is satisfactory," the duty officer said as he handed them the keys. "It is too small for most of the staff, but should suit you fine. There is some food in the kitchen, and fresh linen in the upstairs closet. The court house is just a block away, and Ma'am, the Post Exchange (PX) shops are just a block the other way. The telephone connects with headquarters; should you need anything, just call. MPs patrol the streets for your protection." He bade them a good evening and left.

Neither Ann or George had expected such luxurious accommodation, with everything laid on. They had finished supper and were enjoying a cup of coffee, when there was a knock on the door. A large MP filled the doorway. "Sorry to bother you sir, but we found this man peeking in your windows and trying your door." The MP presented a dirty, disheveled man, who looked vaguely familiar, but George couldn't immediately place him. The man croaked in German, "George, you traitor!"

George thanked the MP, and closed the door. He looked worried as he returned to the kitchen. "Who was that man?" Ann asked. "And how did he know your name and that you were in town?" George just shook his head. "I'm not sure who he is."

In the morning George went to the *Justizpalast* (High Court building). Ann was getting ready to go shopping when the phone rang, It was the duty officer. "Mrs. Hill, I'm sending you a maid, Frieda. She'll do anything you wish."

Ann protested that she didn't need a maid, only somebody to clean and do the wash once a week. "I was just going shopping," Ann added.

"Good," said the duty officer. "Take her with you. She'll help you with the language and your packages."

Ann had just hung up the phone when there was a knock on the door. It was Frieda, a young, bright-looking girl. She was neatly dressed in well-worn clothes, but thin and looked as if she could use a good meal.

Ann explained that she was going shopping, so together they went down the street. At the corner, an MP stopped them. "Take care, Ma'am, and should anyone bother you just blow this whistle, and a member of the force will be right there." Ann thanked him, took the whistle, and they walked on toward the PX stores.

They spent a delightful day shopping for new clothes for both of them. After having lunch in a local cafe they headed home with their purchases. The language barrier had presented few difficulties. Frieda knew some English, and was a great help to Ann in dealing with local merchants. They chatted happily as they walked back to the house.

Suddenly a man stepped out of a doorway and stopped them. He shouted that George was a spy. He said he had been falsely accused of war crimes. Ann didn't know what to do, but told him she would tell George. The man blocked their way, whining and pleading his innocence. Then Ann blew her whistle and an MP hustled the man off. Frieda urged Ann to pay no attention to him. He had been a high-ranking Gestapo, known for his inhumane treatment of the Jews.

George had reported to the *Oberstaatsanwalt*'s (Chief Prosecutor's) office in the morning. They were having serious problems with defendants using false names and claiming no facility in English language. George and the *Oberstaatsanwalt* went to the balcony room overlooking the police lineup. His old friends and acquaintances were there, and he correctly identified them all.

The *Oberstaatsanwalt* turned to George and asked, "Do you know them?"

"Oh yes, every one. They were all fanatical Nazis—so blinded by the glories Hitler promised that they would do anything, including murder."

"But why?"

"Greed, glory, prestige, who knows? If you ask them, separately or collectively, they will tell you that they are innocent and were only obeying orders, for to disobey meant dishonor and/or death."

They walked back to the office. Coffee was served, and they sat around the table. The prosecutor frowned and turned to George. "How did you escape?"

"That's a long story. I was befriended by the head of the *Abwehr*—a very loyal, decent, and courageous anti-Nazi, who lost his life in defending what he believed. Before he was arrested and executed by the Gestapo, he made sure that I was safely out of the country. I owe him a great debt. Perhaps that is one of the reasons why I want see these weak and foolish men punished. Fortunately, the really vicious ones are already dead."

There was silence in the room. George's honesty impressed them all. The *Oberstaatsanwalt* went on. "Do you think this could happen again?"

"Yes, I do, unfortunately, for there will always be the fools—the weak, the gullible, and the greedy, who will fall for glib promises of pie in the sky. We can only hope that the nightmare just ending will never be repeated."

George sat quietly, holding his coffee cup. His thoughts were far away. He thought of Henry. What would he have done? He got up, excused himself and began walking back to the house. In the corridor he was embraced by a French staff officer.

"Georges, where have you been, and how are you? We thought you were dead."

The French officer persisted. "You remember we were at St. Cyr together, before the War?"

George smiled and said yes, this was true. The French officer continued talking. He said he had been captured by the Waffen-SS and had been ill-treated by them. He spat out his hate for the Gestapo. George thought, *I can't tell him the truth.* Fortunately the officer went on to congratulate George on being on the War Trials team. George could see that his double life would continue to cause nothing but trouble.

He walked home and was just opening the door when he was struck on the head from behind. As he fell through the doorway, the attacker screamed, "Take that, for a being traitor!" Ann, who had been making pies in the kitchen, rushed into the hall, rolling pin in hand. Her husband was flat on his face, and his assailant was about to strike him again. Ann rushed at the man and hit him across the face with the rolling pin. The man dropped his club and grabbed his face. Ann blew her whistle. Two MPs appeared, and one grabbed the assailant and handcuffed him; the other bent over George, who was slowly getting to his knees.

George had a large bruise on the back of his head and a bloody nose from falling into the door post. The assailant, with blood running down his face, screamed obscenities and curses at George. George sat up, rubbing the back of his head. Ann and the MP helped him up. He turned and looked at his assailant, and shook his head. "I'm sorry for you, Klaus. You believed all those lies that Hitler told."

"You traitor!" Klaus screamed. "You spy! You never were a true German. I hate you!" He spat at George as the MPs took him away from the house and off to jail.

Ann helped George into the kitchen, pulled out a chair for him at the table and held a cold compress on his bruise. They were talking quietly when a knock on the door made them jump. Ann went to see who it was.

The MP sergeant came into the kitchen. "We're sorry, sir, Ma'am, that this happened. We are under orders to increase our protection. There will be a member of the force on the street at all times. Evidently you and Mrs. Hill are pretty important. Is there anything else that we can do?"

Ann answered, "No, thank you. Mr. Hill will stay home and sleep for the rest of the day, then go back to work tomorrow."

"Very good, Ma'am." He saluted and left.

Ann asked George, "Who was that man who attacked you?"

"Klaus Herzberg, my first cousin. He joined the party as a young boy, and left home early on. He rose through the ranks of the SS-Gestapo until he was second in command in Bohemia, in charge of the deportation of the Austrian and Czech Jews to the death camps. He was as fanatical as Grandfather in his worship of the Party and Hitler. He hated Henry and me. To him, we were not true Germans. He hated mother because she had married an American. Neither Henry nor I could stand him. We considered him a stuck-up prig. Fortunately we saw very little of each other. The last time was at Grandfather's funeral."

George's head began to droop, so Ann gave him two aspirins and helped him into bed. He slept the rest of the afternoon.

• • •

George was busy with interrogations and interviews, but not all the defendants were willing to talk. Some couldn't believe it was happening to them. They considered themselves good Germans who loved the Fatherland. They were only following orders, they said. Many believed that the country had been betrayed after the Great War, and now, betrayed again.

One day, a Russian colonel in full uniform came into the office. He saluted and presented the *Oberstaatsanwalt* with a formal protest, as follows:

The Government of the Soviet Union strongly protests the presence of a member of the fascist Abwehr in office of the Oberstaatsanwalt. The Soviet government feels that such a person compromises the prosecution of fascist war criminals. Therefore, if the situation is not rectified, the Soviet government will be forced to reconsider its position on the War Trials Commission.

A supplemental document was also presented. It was a very detailed description of George's espionage activities with the *Abwehr*, and of his close relationship with Admiral Canaris. The document ended abruptly with their trip to Lisbon. A final sentence said that they did not know what had happened to George. The *Oberstaatsanwalt* called George into his office. "Well," he said, "what are you going to do?"

George replied, "I'm going home. You don't need me any more and my being here will just cause friction. You can inform the Soviet delegation of my resignation. Ann and I will leave by the end of the week."

"Thank you, George. You have been a great help." The *Oberstaatsanwalt* rose and the men shook hands.

George and Ann booked a flight, said goodbye and paid a tearful Frieda her wages. They also thanked the MP's for their protection. Then they flew to London, where they spent a week with the Ann's parents. George's resignation was finally accepted and the department wished them God's speed.

The transport flight to Reykjavík was cold and uncomfortable, but two days with the Pedersons revived their spirits considerably. Then they endured another uncomfortable flight to Idlewild airport.

In the morning they boarded *The Jeffersonian* for the trip west. The following afternoon, the train pulled into Barnesville, where John, Anna, and Emily waited to welcome them home. When Anna threw her arms around Ann and kissed her, Ann seemed a little embarrassed at such a show of emotion. Emily hugged George and Ann, then quietly took Ann's hand as they walked down the platform toward the beginning of a new life.

That night, they all gathered at the Hill's farmhouse for dinner, Grandfather at one end of the table and Grandmother at the other. Marguerite, Kajsa and the aunts sat on one side; John, Anna, Emily, George and Ann on the other. The two young ones, Lars, a sturdy boy of three, and the baby, Anna Katherine (Katie), were asleep upstairs. They all joined hands as Grandfather Hill bowed his head and prayed.

"We thank Thee, Heavenly Father, for uniting our family. We know that Henry will join us soon. We thank thee for our beloved granddaughters, Marguerite, Kajsa, and Ann, and welcome them with loving hearts. We also welcome Anna's dear sisters, and hope through Thy guidance they will find peace and love among us. Heavenly Father, we thank thee for blessing us with Thy abiding love, and with a peace that passeth all understanding. Amen."

17

Requiem

HE AUNTS BOUGHT A LITTLE HOUSE near the center of town. They opened a small, specialty bakery, which was very successful. To the town, they were "the Aunts," highly respected and much-loved members of the community. Their baked goods were in demand for church socials, weddings and other special occasions. On Sunday, after attending the Lutheran church, they could be seen walking, either to John and Anna's or to one of the twin's houses, for dinner. Their eyes, no longer haunted, shone with tranquillity and peace. They never married, perhaps because their experience with the Russian troops had created wounds that were too deep to heal. That part of their lives, they never discussed. Emily loved her aunts, and worked in their bakery store after school and on weekends.

• • •

A German court indicted and tried Klaus Herzberg for war crimes. The court sentenced him to ten years of hard labor. He adamantly refused to admit he had cousins in America, and until his death he stoutly maintained his innocence of all war crimes.

• • •

To everyone's great joy, Kajsa fell in love with young Sam Abbott, whose family ran the local creamery. Sam was a pacifist and had done alternate service in Civilian Public Service Camps and State Mental Hospitals. Sam and Kajsa were married in the Lutheran Church in Barnesville. The Pederson parents made a real vacation of their trip to America. They took a month off for the wedding, and visiting and enjoying

113

their grandchildren. The wedding itself was a time of great joy and celebration. The whole town was invited. Marguerite, Anna, and the Aunts provided a bountiful reception at the Hill's farm.

• • •

George and Henry lived side by side, as if to affirm that they would never be separated again. Occasionally they would talk of shared memories. George was awarded a Presidential Medal for his work with the FBI and the OSS. He refused it, saying that he only did what he had do.

The brothers taught in the local Quaker School: Henry, English and shop courses; George, German and French language. They raised beautiful and responsible families. Marguerite and Kajsa helped with the preschool children, and Marguerite taught Icelandic poetry to the primary grades. Ann was appointed head librarian of the Community Library. During the summer, Henry, Marguerite and their children spent a month in Iceland, occasionally accompanied by Kajsa and her children. George and Ann would often travel to Britain to visit Ann's parents.

• • •

The Hill grandparents had lived long and useful lives. Their dairy farm had survived and prospered during two major wars and a devastating depression. Grandfather Hill's arthritis prevented him from active operation of the farm, so John managed the dairy farm for his father. After Grandmother Hill died of a heart attack, leaving Grandfather alone, John and Anna moved into the homestead to take care of him. Grandfather Hill loved his daughter-in-law Anna—she was very special to him. John sold his house to Kajsa and Sam Abbott. Sam worked for John on the farm. Anna gave daily thanks for her blessings: she lived in a loving community, she adored her husband and he loved her in return; her boys were reunited and lived nearby; Emily was a delight; Anna's sisters were safe and happy. Her Heavenly Father had surely bestowed His blessings on them all.

• • •

Emily sat under a tree and smiled. Her life had been full of surprises. She was lonely when her mother died. Her father was sad, and lonely too. Often, as a little girl, she evaded her nanny and ran across the fields to

Grandmother's house, there to be embraced by loving arms. All that changed when her father married Anna. Such a warm and loving person, and so wonderful to have a caring mother again. Then there was her new, older brother Henry. She loved him dearly and would tag along after him whenever she could. Her mother told her about a second older brother, George, who lived in Germany.

One morning Emily found her mother crying in the kitchen because her father had died. Emily comforted her mother the very best she could. Anna couldn't go the funeral, but had sent Henry in her place.

Another surprise had been Henry's new wife from Iceland. But the biggest surprise was the day that George walked into the kitchen. Here was her other brother, and he looked just like Henry! Then Henry came in and the twins stood on either side their mother. Happiness and joy shone in their faces, for it had been a long, long time since they were all together. Emily looked at them and knew she could tell her twin brothers apart.

The next big surprise was not George's new wife, for somehow she expected that. It was the coming of the aunts. Two very frightened, timid ladies with haunted eyes, who needed to be loved and cherished. These were her mother's sisters, but not really like her mother. Emily's heart went out to them.

The afternoon shadows were beginning to lengthen. Emily sat under the tree waiting for her brothers. The years had been kind to her: she had worked with the Aunts in her spare time, earning money for college; she graduated from Antioch with a degree in Business and a minor in Psychology; she married a young man from town. It was a happy marriage, albeit of only a year, which had tragically been cut short when he died in a farm accident and left Emily with a baby boy, Little John. She continued to live in her small house near the bakery. This was very convenient for the Aunts. Emily took over the accounting side of their business, and did most of the bookkeeping at home. After Grandfather Hill died, she sold her house and moved into the homestead with her parents. This delighted Anna, for now she had Little John to care for. Little John adored his grandfather Big John, who took the boy with him whenever he could—in the truck, on the wagon, and sometimes on the tractor.

• • •

When Anna and John passed away, Emily lived alone in the old house. She didn't mind, for it was full of wonderful memories. Emily bought the aunts' bakery when they retired, and operated the business successfully for twenty years before she sold it. Little John grew up and eventually married one of Kajsa and Sam's granddaughters, and together they ran a very prosperous farm of their own. With the passing of Marguerite and Ann, the twins sold their houses and moved into the old homestead. Emily was only too glad to share the house with her brothers. They were the last of a generation.

• • •

Henry and George walked slowly up the hill to the cemetery. Their step was still strong, although they had passed their eightieth birthday. They were the elders of the Quaker Meeting now. They had lived long and wonderful lives. They entered the cemetery and walked among the graves. To their left, up the hill, were the graves of their grandparents and the Aunts. A little way along was their mother's stone between her two husbands, Peter and John. To their right were the graves of their beloved wives, Marguerite and Ann.

They walked to a nearby bench and sat down. They were the last of the family who had lived through those terrible years of separation, sacrifice, and struggle. Years when they had been forced by circumstance to follow different paths. Years which they hoped would never be forgotten, or repeated. Their experiences and adventures were almost unbelievable. The story had to be told, but even so, they hesitated. Would anyone believe them? They heard their Grandfather's voice: "Wait upon the Lord, and He will show thee the Way."

They sat in peaceful silence, meditating, and only speaking occasionally. They finally agreed to record all their experiences—feelings, joys, and sorrows—with the understanding that nothing would be published until after they had passed on.

The sun slipped behind the trees, and the shadows lengthened over the cemetery. A feeling of peace and love filled their hearts. They rose and walked along the path out of the cemetery, patting the family headstones as they passed. They turned and walked slowly down the hill, and saw their dear sister Emily waiting for them. They told her of their decision. She hugged them both, for she loved them dearly. Then she took the inside arm of each twin, and they walked slowly home for supper.

EPILOGUE
Personal Observations

AFTER 63 YEARS, I revisited Germany and saw for myself how much has changed. I was struck by the fact that the years from 1930 to 1945 are completely ignored. Visiting with people who lived through the Nazi period, I discovered that nobody wants to talk about it. It's as if they have blocked out that period of history. No one will admit to being a Party member, yet in order to survive those years, one had to be. There are a few remnants of the West Wall fortifications, but very few other reminders of the Nazi period. Concentration camps are now museums, haunted by ghosts. Towns which once had thriving Jewish populations now have none. A plaque hangs on the wall of an empty synagogue listing the names of those who perished, or were deported. You can't blame *everyone*, but the evil that swept the land like a plague effected *everyone*, and so *everyone* is responsible to see that the nightmare never happens again.

In the United States, the scars of the Great Depression run deep: the rationing and poverty are still remembered. In the minds of many seniors and veterans lurks the fear that it could all happen again. In the homes of many a survivor of those years, there are stockpiles of food and other supplies—often up to a year's worth! The country participated in and survived a terrible period of military conflict and eventually emerged as a superpower, a role that was new and with which it's administration and leadership were unfamiliar. As the country demonstrated—with the bombing of Hiroshima and Nagasaki—their progress with nuclear weapon technology, and willingness to use it, terrified the world. With it, the United States entered a new and different era of their history.

GLOSSARY

Abwehr – literally means "defense," the *Abwehr* was the counterintelligence branch of the high command of the *Wehrmacht* or German Armed Forces and was headquartered at the OKW Building, in Berlin. Though disapproving of aspects of the Nazi regime, Wilhelm Canaris rose under Hitler to become Admiral of the German navy and chief of the *Abwehr*. Associated with the 1944 bomb plot against Hitler, he was arrested, imprisoned and hanged.

Auschwitz – (Pol., Oswiecim), largest Nazi concentration and extermination camp, located 60 km west of Krakow. Auschwitz was both an extensive Nazi concentration camp, as well as the largest death camp at which Jews were exterminated by means of poison gas. In March 1941, Himmler ordered the construction of a second, much larger section of the camp, Auschwitz Birkenau, which was located at a distance 3 km from the original camp. In nearby Monowitz (Pol., Monowice), a third camp was built which was called Auschwitz III (Buna-Monowitz). Auschwitz III (Buna-Monowitz and the other forty-five subcamps) was made up of mainly forced labor camps. Auschwitz was the largest graveyard in human history. The number of Jews murdered in the gas chambers of Birkenau is estimated at up to one and a half million people.

CCC – (Civilian Conservation Corps) established work camps during the depression for unemployed me who undertook conservation work, and built facilities in state and national parks. These camps were closed down when the United States entered the Second World War.

Chamberlain, Neville (1869–1940) – British Prime Minister, elected in May 1937, succeeding Stanley Baldwin. Three years later he resigned over criticism triggered by Britain's withdrawal from Norway but largely informed by public disenchantment with his prewar foreign policy—commonly associated with appeasement—a popular policy in Britain in the 1930's. Chamberlain saw it as his mission to prevent war with Germany and, if that could not be achieved, to postpone hostilities as long as possible in order to give maximum time for rearmament. In 1939, in relation to the British guarantee of Poland's border, Chamberlain saw that appeasement was at an end. In May 1940 he resigned to make way for Winston Churchill and died shortly afterwards. His honorable intentions were quickly erased from the public mind once Britain and Germany were at war. Chamberlain was seen as a gullible English gentleman who had been totally outmaneuvered by a ruthless Führer.

Chancellor – head of the German government; the equivalent of the Prime Minister of Great Britain, or the President of the United States of America.

Churchill, Sir Winston Leonard Spencer (1874 – 1965) – British Prime Minister from May 1940 till July 1945 and again from 1951 – 55. Churchill became the wartime Prime Minister as a result of his speeches of supreme eloquence that defied the Nazis and reflected the emotional mood of the nation and he became the spirit of British resistance incarnate. He became a historical figure of significance for the first time in 1911—as 1st Lord of the Admiralty and his modernization of the British fleet played a significant role in the successful outcome for Britain in the 1914 – 18 war. Churchill retained a seat in the House of Commons until 1964, a year before his death.

CO – Conscientious objectors who claimed religious grounds for their pacifism were classified 4E by the draft boards.

CPS – (Civilian Public Service) reopened old CCC camps all over the United States for Conscientious Objectors who were put to work in state hospitals, were made subjects in medical experiments and trials for hepatitis/jaundice research and soil conservation. CPS internees were detained for almost a year after the end of WWII and were not released until after all US armed forces personnel had returned home.

FBI – Federal Bureau of Investigation is a US organization primarily concerned with internal security or counterintelligence operations. It is a branch of the Department of Justice.

der Führer – literally means "the Leader" and is the title Adolf Hitler assumed in 1933 when he became Chancellor.

Gestapo – abbreviation of *Geheime Staatspolizei* who were the secret police of the German Third Reich. Founded in 1933, under Herman (Wilhelm) Göring

1893–1946, who reorganized the Prussian plain clothes police as the Gestapo, setting up concentration camps for political, racial and religious suspects. The Gestapo came under the control of Himmler in 1936 and were renamed as the *Schutsstaffel* or SS who were also Hitler's protective force or body guards. The SD or *Sicherheitsdienst* were a Security Service of the SS, under the leadership of Reinhard Heydrich whose purpose was to supply intelligence for Gestapo operations. The Waffen-SS were the fully-equipped army corps of the secret police, which fought on both eastern and western fronts.

Gestapo-SS – see Gestapo.

Göbbels, (Paul) Joseph (1897–1945) – Nazi politician, born in Rheydt, Germany. A deformed foot absolved him from military service, and he attended several universities. He became Hitler's enthusiastic supporter, and was appointed head of the Ministry of Public Enlightenment and Propaganda (1933). A bitter anti-Semite, his gift of mob oratory made him a powerful exponent of the more radical aspects of Nazi philosophy. Wartime conditions greatly expanded his responsibilities and power, and by 1943, while Hitler was running the war, Göbbels was virtually running the country. He retained Hitler's confidence to the last, and in the Berlin bunker he and his wife committed suicide, after taking the lives of their six children.

Godesberg Conference – Historians have proposed that the Godesberg Conference of 22–23 September 1938, was the occasion of an explicit "deal" between the British prime minister, Neville Chamberlain, and Adolf Hitler whereby the latter would leave western Europe and its colonies alone in exchange for a free hand in the east where he could concentrate his energies on destroying the Soviet Union. Thus, the British guarantee to Poland at the end of March 1939 was a response not to the German destruction of Czechoslovakia but perhaps to Chamberlain's fear that Hitler had reneged on the Godesberg deal and was contemplating military action against the West. The Polish guarantee was designed to persuade Hitler to redirect his priorities towards southeast Europe. The scheme failed and for a long time, after the outbreak of war in September 1939, British leaders remained hopeful of reestablishing an accord with Hitler. At Godesberg, Hitler had harangued Chamberlain and after he had forced him to agree to transmit his new demands to the Czech government, he abruptly adopted an expansive and conciliatory mood and began talking about an Anglo-German rapprochement. In particular he told Chamberlain: "we will not stand in the way of your pursuit of your non-European interests and you may without harm let us have a free hand on the European continent in central and South-East Europe." The "deal" (if there was one) could certainly help to explain British behavior at Munich but also the seeming British turnabout in the wake of the mid- March Nazi annexation of Moravia and Bohemia. When Chamberlain learned, on March 17, 1939, that Hitler had agreed to award Ruthenia (the largely Ukrainian parts of the by now ex-Czechoslovakia) to Hungary—something he had refused to do at the time of the Munich conference—this suggested to Chamberlain that Hitler no longer intended to strike first in the east, i.e., into the Ukraine, but that he might, as diplomats had been warning since at least December of the previous year, be turning west. So Chamberlain's sudden resolve was quite possibly motivated not by Hitler's cynical violation of the Munich agreement, but by his betrayal of the Godesberg "deal." Consequently the subsequent guarantee to Poland is seen as less an act of diplomatic firmness than a desperate attempt to induce Hitler to return to his previous understanding. It is an interesting theory and certainly not inherently implausible. Once again, however, it is a theory that depends on the unproven thesis of an explicit Hitler-Chamberlain deal.

Göring, Hermann (Wilhelm) (1893 – 1946) – Nazi politico-military leader, born in Rosenheim, Germany. In the 1914 – 18 war he fought on the Western Front, then transferred to the air force, and commanded the famous 'Death Squadron.' In 1922 he joined the Nazi Party and was given command of the Hitler storm troopers. He became president of the Reichstag in 1932, and joined the Nazi government in 1933. He founded the Gestapo, setting up the concentration camps for political, racial, and religious suspects. In 1940 he became economic dictator of Germany, and was made Marshal of the Reich, the first and only holder of the rank. As the war went against Germany, his prestige waned. In 1944 he attempted a palace revolution, was condemned to death, but escaped, to be captured by US troops. In 1946 he was sentenced to death at the Nuremberg War Crimes Trial, but before his execution could take place he committed suicide.

Heydrich, Reinhard, nickname the Hangman (1904–42) – Nazi politician and
deputy-chief of the Gestapo, born in Halle, Germany. He joined the violent
anti-Weimar 'Free Corps' (1918), and served in the navy (1922–31), quitting
to join the Nazi Party. He rose to be second-in-command of the secret police,
and was charged with subduing Hitler's war-occupied countries, which he
did by ordering mass executions. In 1941 he was made deputy-protector of
Bohemia and Moravia, but next year was struck down by Czech assassins. In
the murderous reprisals, Lidice village was razed and every man put to death.

Himmler, Heinrich (1900–45) German Nazi leader and chief of police, born in
Munich, Germany. He joined the Nazi Party in 1925, and in 1929 was made
head of the SS (*Schutzstaffel*, protective force), which he developed from
Hitler's personal bodyguard into a powerful Party weapon. He also directed
the secret police (Gestapo), and initiated the systematic liquidation of Jews.
In 1943 he became minister of the interior, and in 1944 commander-in-
chief of the home forces. He was captured by the Allies, and committed
suicide in Lüneburg.

Hindenburg, Paul (Ludwig Hans Anton von Beneckendorff und) von (1847–
1934) – German general and president (1925–34), born in Posnan, Poland
(formerly, Posen, Prussia). Educated at Wahlstatt and Berlin, he fought in
the Franco-Prussian War (1870–1), rose to the rank of general (1903), and
retired in 1911. Recalled at the outbreak of World War I, he won victories
over the Russians (1914–15), but was forced to direct the German retreat
on the Western Front (to the Hindenburg line). A national hero, he became
the second president of the German Republic in 1925. He was reelected in
1932, and in 1933 appointed Hitler as chancellor.

Hitler Youth – or Hitler Jugend, the Nazi equivalent of the Boy Scouts. All boys
had to join; a girls section was als developed.

Hoover, Herbert (Clark) (1874–1964) – US statesman and 31st president (1929–
33), born in West Branch, IA. He studied at Stanford, then worked abroad as
an engineer. During and after World War I he was associated with the relief
of distress in Europe. In 1921 he became secretary of commerce, and in 1928
received the Republican Party's presidential nomination. As president, his
opposition to direct governmental assistance for the unemployed after the
world slump of 1929 made him unpopular, and he was beaten by Roosevelt

in 1932. He assisted Truman with the various American-European economic relief programs which followed World War II.

Kaiser – title assumed by the Prussian King, William (Wilhelm) I, following the unification of Germany and the creation of the German Second Empire. His grandson, Wilhelm II ruled until his enforced abdication in 1918.

Leopold III (1901–83) King of Belgium (1934–51), born in Brussels. He was the son of Albert I, and he married Princess Astrid of Sweden in 1926. On his own authority he ordered the capitulation of his army to the Nazis (1940), thus opening the way to Dunkirk. He then remained a prisoner in his own palace at Laeken until 1944, and afterwards in Austria. On returning to Belgium in 1945, he was finally forced to abdicate in favor of his son, Baudouin.

Maginot Line – a line of French defensive fortifications, named after the French Minister of War, Andre Maginot, built along its northeastern frontier from Switzerland to Luxembourg to protect against German invasion, completed in 1936.

Majdanek – Concentration camp run by the Waffen-SS. (Konzentrationslager der Waffen-SS Lublin). Majdanek was located in a suburb of Lublin, Poland, and was called the Majdan Tatarski camp, or Majdanek for short. It was established on the orders of Heinrich Himmler, following an agreement with the Wehrmacht under which some Soviet prisoners of war would be handed over to the SS and put at the disposal of the program for the "Germanization" of the east. Its function was to destroy enemies of the Third Reich and to take part in the extermination of the Jews and the deportation and "resettlement" of the inhabitants of the Zamosc region. Close to 500,000 persons, from 28 countries and belonging to 54 different nationalities, passed through Majdanek. Of these, according to current estimates, some 360,000 perished. Sixty percent of them died as a result of the conditions in the camp—starvation, exhaustion, disease, and beatings—and 40% were put to death in gas chambers or executed.

NSDAP – *National Sozialistische Deutsche Arbeiterpartei* or Nazi for short was the National Socialist German Workers' Party and the official name of Hitler's political party.

OKW – *Oberkommando der Wehrmacht* the headquarters of the Commander-in-Chief of the German Armed Forces in Berlin.

OSS – Office of Strategic Services. The OSS was the predecessor of the Central Intelligence Agency or CIA.

Papen, Franz von (1879–1969) – Politician, born in Werl, Germany. He was military attaché in Mexico and Washington, chief-of-staff with a Turkish army, and took to Centre Party politics. As Hindenburg's chancellor (1932) he suppressed the Prussian Socialist government, and as Hitler's vice-chancellor (1933–4) signed a concordat with Rome. He later became ambassador to Austria (1936–8) and Turkey (1939–44). Taken prisoner in 1945, he was acquitted at the Nuremberg Trials.

Paulus, Friedrich (1890–1957) – German soldier and tank specialist, born in Breitenau, Germany. He served in World War I, and by 1940 was deputy chief of the general staff. As commander of the 6th Army he led the attack on Stalingrad (1942), but was trapped in the city by a Russian counterattack. Totally cut off, he and his troops held out for three months before capitulating in February 1943. Released from captivity in 1953, he became a lecturer on military affairs under the East German Communist government.

PX – Post Exchange shops or stores established for military personnel and their families. Prices for merchandise were tax free and much lower than those for the same or similar merchandise on the open market.

Reich – German term used to describe the German Empire. The Holy Roman Empire (962–1806) is regarded as the First Reich; Unified Germany after 1870, is regarded as the Second Reich (Kaiserreich); and the enlarged Germany envisioned by Hitler after 1933 is the Third Reich.

Roosevelt, Franklin D(ellano), nickname FDR (1882–1945) - US statesman and 32nd president (1933–45), born in Hyde Park, NY. He became a lawyer (1907), a New York State senator (1910–13), and assistant secretary of the navy 1913–20). He was Democratic candidate for the vice-presidency in 1920, and Governor of New York (1928–32), although stricken with paralysis (polio) in 1921. He met the economic crisis with his 'New Deal' for national recovery (1933), and became the only president to be reelected three times. He strove in vain to ward off war, modified the USA's neutrality to favor the Allies, and was brought in by Japan's action at Pearl Harbor

(1941). He met with Churchill and Stalin at Teheran (1943) and Yalta (1945), but died at Warm Springs, GA, where he had long gone for treatment, three weeks before the German surrender.

SA – members of the Nazi Party, also known as the "brown shirts, " they were the semi-military storm troopers which rivaled the German army. Their power was destroyed when members of their leadership plotting a coup were discovered and executed by Hitler in 1934.

SD – see Gestapo

Spartacists – left-wing revolutionary faction *Spartakusbund* led by Rosa Luxemburg and Karl Liebknecht (1871–1919) which supported the Russian Revolution in 1917, advocated ending the war and promoted a German Socialist Revolution. In 1918 the Spartacists became the German Communist Party.

SS – see Gestapo

Treaty of Versailles – signed on June 28, 1919, officially bringing World War I to an end. The Treaty declared Germany guilty of causing the war, and made provision for the trial of the former Kaiser and other war leaders; imposed heavy reparations payments in "compensation for all damage done to the civilian population of the Allied and Associated Powers and to their property during the period of the belligerency of each;" limited the German army and navy to nominal strength. The army was limited to 100,000 men with no conscription, no tanks, no heavy artillery, and no poison gas supplies. The navy was limited to vessels under 100,000 tons, with no submarines. Moreover "the armed forces of Germany must not include any military or naval airforces;" returned Alsace and Lorraine to France, ceded parts of Germany to Poland, and provided for the Allied occupation of the Rhineland; turned most German colonies into mandates of the League of Nations, which was established by the Treaty.

Tiso, Josef (1887 – 1947) – Slovak priest and politician who ruled Slovakia from 1939–45, as a Nazi satellite. Even when informed that deported Slovakian Jews were being exterminated, he did not intervene. He did grant exemption from deportation to 1,100 wealthy Jews who agreed to baptism. In 1945 he fled, but was captured, tried and executed.

Treblinka – Extermination camp in the northeastern part of the General Gouvernement was situated in a sparsely populated area near Malkinia, a railway station on the main Warsaw – Bialystok line. A penal camp, known as Treblinka I, had been set up nearby in 1941. The mass extermination program at Treblinka went into effect on July 23, 1942, and the first transports to reach the camp were made up of Jews from the Warsaw ghetto—residents of the General Gouvernement. The mass extermination program continued until April 1943, after which only a few isolated transports arrived; the camp had fulfilled its function. A total of 870,000 people had been murdered there.

Tsar or Czar – derived from the Latin word *Caesar*, and the title used by the rulers of Russia from 1547 until 1721. It remained in common use until the Revolution in 1917, although the official title of the ruler from 1721–1917 was Emperor.

Vichy Government of France – formed when the German Army occupied Paris on June 14, 1940, and it became apparent that the German western offensive could not be halted. French Prime Minister, Paul Reynaud, suggested the government move to French territories in North Africa. Instead, his vice-premier, Henri-Philippe Pétain, insisted that the government should remain in France and seek an armistice. Reynaud resigned and Pétain was appointed as France's new premier. He immediately began negotiations with Adolf Hitler and on June 22, signed an armistice with Germany. The terms of the agreement divided France into occupied and unoccupied zones. The Germans would directly control three-fifths of the country, an area that included northern and western France and the entire Atlantic coast. The remaining section of the country would be administered by the French government at Vichy under Pétain.

Other provisions of the armistice included the surrender of all Jews living in France to the Germans. The Vichy regime deported over 70,000 Jews to Germany and sent 650,000 workers to Germany to help their war effort. The French Army was disbanded except for a force of 100,000 men to maintain domestic order. The 1.5 million French soldiers captured by the Germans were to remain prisoners of war. The French government also agreed to stop members of its armed forces from leaving the country and instructed its citizens not to fight against the Germans. Finally, France had to pay the occupation costs of the German troops.

Over the next four years, Pétain led the right-wing government of Vichy France. The state was under German control but tried to maintain the fiction of independence with a French administration—especially for police and justice. The famous revolutionary principles of "Liberty, Equality, Fraternity," were replaced by "Work, Family, Fatherland."

To counter the Vichy regime, General Charles de Gaulle created France Libre (Free France) and established a government in exile headquartered in London. Although Metropolitan France (the home territory of a sovereign state) was under German control, pretending to be independent, parts of the Empire such as French Equatorial Africa, New Caledonia, French Polynesia and St. Pierre and Miquelon, rallied to de Gaulle's call. In June 1941, the British Army and Free French forces invaded Syria and Lebanon, capturing Damascus on June 17, and after the D-Day landings took place on June 6, 1944, the Maquis (French underground organization) and other resistance groups emerged to help in the liberation of their country.

Following the Allied invasion of France, Pétain and his ministers fled to Germany and established a government in exile at Sigmaringen. In 1945 the leaders of the Vichy government were arrested and some were executed for war crimes. Pétain was sentenced to death but the sentence was commuted to life imprisonment. Others fled or went into hiding.

Waffen-SS – Perhaps the most infamous and least understood organizations of WWII, the SS was not a monolithic "Black Corps" of goose-stepping Gestapo, but a complex political and military organization made up of three separate and distinct branches which were related but equally unique in their functions and goals. The Allgemeine-SS (General SS) was the main branch and served a political and administrative role. The SS-Totenkopfverbande (SS Deaths Head Organization) and later the Waffen-SS (Armed SS), were the other two branches that formed the organization. The Waffen-SS, formed in 1940, was the true military formation of the organization. Formed from the SS-Verfungstruppe after the Campaign in France in 1940, the Waffen-SS would become an elite military formation of nearly 600,000 men by the time WWII was over. Its units would spearhead some of the most crucial battles of WWII while its men would shoulder some of the most difficult and daunting combat operations of all the units in the German military. The Waffen-SS is sometimes thought of as the fourth branch of the German Wehrmacht (Heer, Luftwaffe, Kriegsmarine) as in the field it came under the direct tactical control of the OKW, although this notion is technically incorrect as strategic control remained within the hands of the SS. To this day the actions of the Waffen-SS and its former members are vilified for ultimately being a part of the larger structure of the political Allgemeine-SS, regardless of the fact that the Waffen-SS was a front line combat organization. *See also* Gestapo.

Wannsee – the location of a retreat/conference held on January 30, 1942. At Hitler's request, Reinhard Heydrich, Deputy Chief of the SS, convened a meeting of representatives of the various ministries and agencies of the SS and SD in the Berlin suburb of Wannsee to discuss the "final solution of the European Jewish problem."

Wilhelm II (of Germany), known as Kaiser Wilhelm (1859–1941) – German emperor and king of Prussia (1888 – 1918), born in Potsdam, Germany, the eldest son of Frederick III (1831 – 88) and Victoria (the daughter of Britain's Queen Victoria), and grandson of Emperor William I. He dismissed Bismark (1890), and began a long period of personal rule, displaying a bellicose attitude in international affairs. He pledged full support to Austria-Hungary after the assassination of Archduke Francis Ferdinand at Sarajevo (1914), but then made apparent efforts to prevent the escalation of the resulting international crisis. During the war he became a mere figurehead, and when the German armies collapsed, and US President Wilson refused to negotiate while he remained in power, he abdicated and fled the country. He settled at Doorn, in The Netherlands, living as a country gentleman.

BIBLIOGRAPHY

Abel, T. (1965). *The Nazi movement*. New York, NY: Atherton Press.

Allen, F.L. (1952). *The big change*. New York, NY: Harper & Brothers.

———— (1939). *Since yesterday, 1929–1939*. New York, NY: Harper & Row.

Ayer, E. (2000). *Parallel journeys*. New York, NY: Aladdin.

Berton, P. (1 99 1). *The great depression, 1929–1939*. Toronto, ON: Penguin.

Boardman F.W. (1967). *The thirties, America and the great depression*. New York, NY: Henry Z. Walck, Inc.

Broadfoot, B. (1975). *Ten lost years 1929–1939*. Don Mills, ON: Paper Jacks.

Crystal, D. (Ed.) (1994). *The Cambridge biographical encyclopedia*. Cambridge, UK: Cambridge University Press.

Elkinton, K.W. 1933–41). *The journals of Katherine W Elkinton, 1933–1941*. Unpublished journals of the author's mother.

Encyclopedia Britannica Inc. (1975). *Britannica atlas*. Chicago, IL: Encyclopedia Britannica Inc.

Lynton, M. (1 998). *Accidental journey: A Cambridge internee's memoir of world war II*. Woodstock, NY: The Overlook Press.

Magnusson, M. (Ed.) (1990). *Cambridge biographical dictionary*. New York, NY: Cambridge University Press.

Mosse, G.L. (1972). *The crisis of German ideology*. New York, NY: Grosset & Dunlap.

Shirer, W.L. (1995). *The rise and fall of the third reich, Volumes I & 11*. London, UK: The Folio Society.

———— (1984) *The nightmare years, 1930–1940*. Boston, MA: Little, Brown and Company.

———— (1969). *The collapse of the third republic: An inquiry into the fall of France in 1940*. New York, NY: Simon & Shuster.

———— (1961). The rise and fall of Adolf Hitler. Toronto, ON: Scholastic Book Services.

Strong, C.F. (1967). The twentieth century and the contemporary world. London, UK: University of London Press.

Times Books (1996). The Times atlas of the world, compact edition. London, UK: Times Books.

Vogt, H. (1965). The burden of guilt: A short history of Germany, 1914 – 1945. Toronto, ON: Oxford University Press.

Walker, P. (Ed.) (1995). Chronology of the twentieth century. Oxford, UK: Helion Publishing Ltd.

ABOUT THE AUTHOR

PETER W. ELKINGTON HAS BEEN DESCRIBED AS A CHRONICLER, and a teller of tales. He comes from a long line of storytellers. His grandmother, and her mother before her, would have the grandchildren gather around for a story hour in the evening. His mother, Katharine, was an extraordinary storyteller. She told tales, some true, some fictitious, that were both vivid and realistic. Peter W. Elkington has continued this tradition by writing and telling stories based on historical events or happenings, or sheer fiction.

Peter lives in Revelstoke, British Columbia. *Twins* is his seventh book and his fifth volume of fiction. During the summer months he travels widely, gathering new material for future books.

Other Books by Peter W. Elkington

fiction
The Road, 1994
The Road West, 1995
The Roots of the Road, 1997
Once There Was A Railroad, 2001

philosophy
We Shall Overcome, 1996

biography
Katharine Wistar Elkinton, 2000